*A Candlelight Ecstasy Romance*®

## SHE WANTED HIM. . . .

There was no question about that. And now she knew how much he wanted her.

"Oh, Penny . . . Penny," he moaned. "My beautiful girl."

No, it wasn't real. Joel Sanborne could not be saying those words to her and if he were, he could not be meaning them. Her body thrilled beneath his hands, desperate to fulfill the restlessness his touch had created while, against her own will, she heard her voice say no, no, and no again. . . .

## A CANDLELIGHT ECSTASY ROMANCE ®

# A SILENT WONDER

*Samantha Hughes*

**A CANDLELIGHT ECSTASY ROMANCE ®**

Published by
Dell Publishing Co., Inc.
1 Dag Hammarskjold Plaza
New York, New York 10017

Dell ® TM 681510, Dell Publishing Co., Inc.

Candlelight Ecstasy Romance®, 1,203,540, is a registered
trademark of Dell Publishing Co., Inc.,
New York, New York.

ISBN: 0-440-18409-6

Printed in the United States of America
First printing—March 1983

To Our Readers:

We have been delighted with your enthusiastic response to Candlelight Ecstasy Romances® and we thank you for the interest you have shown in this exciting series.

In the upcoming months we will continue to present the distinctive, sensuous love stories you have come to expect only from Ecstasy. We look forward to bringing you many more books from your favorite authors and also the very finest work from new authors of contemporary romantic fiction.

As always, we are striving to present the unique absorbing love stories that you enjoy most—books that are more than ordinary romance.

Your suggestions and comments are always welcome. Please write to us at the address below.

Sincerely,

The Editors
Candlelight Romances
1 Dag Hammarskjold Plaza
New York, New York 10017

# CHAPTER ONE

Penelope Phillips shifted the tan canvas bag, which was bulging with two weeks worth of unedited television scripts, and sniffed the delicious sea air. So far they had not yet caught sight of the ocean, but the salt was definitely in the air and it was a good fifteen degrees cooler here in Marblehead than it had been in Boston. Not to mention the one-hundred-degree temperatures they had suffered through before leaving New York City. Thank God she was out of New York City for a couple of weeks. As much as she loved the Big Apple most of the time, in late August it was definitely not the place to be.

"I love it, I love it, I love it!" Irene Sullivan, one of the new young stars of *Dream of Life* hopped along next to Penny. Her languid gray eyes were more open and alert than Penny had ever seen them, and she grinned at Irene's uninhibited enthusiasm. Although Irene at twenty-three was only four years younger than Penny, Penny had the distinct feeling that the disheveled little blonde had adopted her as a mother figure. Ever since the television show's director, Max Frost, had announced that Penny would be the assistant director for the daytime soap opera's "remote"—industry jargon for a location shoot—Irene had been acting as if she and Penny were best of friends.

Penny could feel the muscles in the back of her calves tighten as she trudged up the steep, narrow, winding streets of Marblehead. Irene continued to let out whoops of enthusiasm as they passed by the perfectly appointed colonial homes lining tiny streets that wound like a maze through the old fishing village. Penny's response, though less vociferous, was equally enthusiastic, for walking through Marblehead was like making a journey into Revolutionary War days. The houses were mostly tiny, some with white picket fences and little gates overrun with creeping roses. Occasionally they would pass a more elaborate brick mansion and pause to read the plaque that identified the home as that of "Ebenezer Raleigh" or some such colonial, salty-sounding person. Many of the houses dated back to the 1680s. But as far as Penny was concerned, the really incredible thing about the old homes in Marblehead was that people still lived in them. They were not simply museum pieces for a curious public. The old town was very much alive.

"I still think we should share a room, Pen," Irene urged in her throaty voice as they came to an intersection that led them back onto the main shopping street of the old village.

Penny shook her head and smiled. Irene was clearly proof that one cannot tell a book by its cover. With her sultry blond beauty, hoarse voice, and siren-sloppy clothes she emitted blatant sexual signals. Yet, as Penny had learned sitting next to her on the flight up from New York City, Irene was as naïve as a baby. She had been born and raised in New York, and this trip to colonial New England seemed to pose a problem for her. Irene was frightened. That was why she kept insisting that she and Penny share a room.

"The New England Yacht Club . . ." Irene's voice was filled with dismay. "It sounds awfully stuffy. Like it'll be full of Boston blue-blood people . . . isn't that what you call them?"

Penny laughed and put down her canvas bag to rest. "You'll be so busy working you won't have time to worry about what color blood the other guests have. Irene, your imagination is getting the better of you. You are not the heroine of a gothic novel. A fat, gray-haired lady with a lorgnette is not going to put poison in your tea, nor is a handsome, dark-haired man with a limp going to seduce you against your will."

Irene giggled. "I didn't know you had such a good sense of humor. Back at the studio you're always so serious."

Penny raised one hand to shield her eyes from the sun and squinted through her glasses at a group of inquisitive tourists forming around Max and the other stars of *Dream of Life*.

"Irene, I need to be by myself. We'll have dinner together, of course, but I'm going to need every minute I can grab to study scripts and keep on top of things. I still can't believe Max chose me over all the other assistant directors to go on remote. Not that I don't deserve it! God knows, I've been hanging around the studio longer than Ted or Allan. If I could get one good film clip out of this . . ."

Penny broke off and ran a pale, slender hand through the sandy hair that fell to her shoulders in a blunt, no-nonsense cut.

"Anyhow"—Penny hoisted the bulging bag of scripts to her shoulder—"I have tons of work to do. Max wants me to edit the first three scripts before we begin shooting. You figure it out."

"I think it's harder being a director than an actress," Irene said, and smiled understandingly.

"A *woman* director," Penny said pointedly.

"Yeah, well at least you're young," Irene said.

"Sometimes," Penny mused with a sigh, "I think I'd have a better chance if I were old and wore brown suits and oxfords. Thank God I'm not beautiful like you and Tippy, or I'd never stand a chance."

"But . . ." Irene began to protest, but Penny rambled on.

"I'm not beautiful, Irene . . . and I wouldn't have it any other way. I'll tell you something. I don't need to wear these glasses all the time. Only for reading. But I wear them basically because I think they give me credibility. You know? They tell the world: This is a serious young woman!"

Irene giggled and tossed her blond hair back from her face.

9

"You are serious. It took me two months down at the studio to get up the nerve to sit with you during coffee breaks."

Max Frost, the show's director, intercepted them and hurried Irene off to be interviewed and photographed in front of one of the landmark buildings on the main street. Poor Max looked frazzled already. Penny hung back, watching him corral his other female star, the fans' favorite heroine, Tippy Malone. Tippy had been on *Dream of Life* since she was a child, and though she professed to being in her early thirties, Penny suspected she was a good deal older. Both of the female stars were petite, and that, thought Penny, made things both easier and more difficult for her. On the one hand Penny's five feet ten inches gave her a sense of authority over the other two women, but on the other hand she often felt like a bungling oaf around them.

Damn, she wished Max had arranged for her to go on ahead to the New England Yacht Club so that she could get settled in her room and begin working on the scripts. But as fond as she was of Max, he was not the world's most organized person, and now here she was, stuck waiting around while the press and photographers did their work. She turned to gaze wistfully into a shop window filled with delicate Victorian clothes—dresses, nightgowns, lacy pantaloons and petticoats. She wondered what it would be like to wear one of the full-skirted petticoats that were all the rage this summer. Everything was white; everything was Victorian. It was very curious how sensual those Victorian fashions were.

"Pretty sexy, wouldn't you say?"

Penny froze at the familiar sound of the deep, melodious voice. She swallowed and tried to think of something glib to combat the dark, flirtatious eyes that always seemed to bore right through her. Of all the actors and actresses in the cast, the only one to make her feel totally inadequate and flimsy was Joel Sanborne, the show's most popular and charming villain.

"I'm especially partial to that high-necked blouse with the

lacy cuffs. Why do you suppose these modest Victorian styles are such a turn-on?"

Joel moved closer, grazing her breast slightly with the sleeve of his beige raw silk jacket. He was dressed for the sun in crisp white pants that tied at the waist and a pale blue tennis shirt that accentuated the smooth, lean muscles of his upper arms and clung tightly to his chest. As usual he was wearing tennis shoes. Penny tried to think if she had ever seen him in anything but tennis shoes.

"A lot is left to the imagination." Penny continued staring in the window. "They're very pretty . . . delicate. All the things a woman is supposed to be."

"Yes." Joel seemed to shift closer to her. "You know, I think it's great that Max decided you should assist on the remote." Joel fell into stride next to her as she began walking toward the group of actors and photographers.

"You do?" Penny looked skeptical. As usual, whenever they exchanged words she felt tight and protective, anticipating some slick remark from him or some of the well-known Sanborne temperament.

"Sure," he said, smiling down at her. "Those other ADs are monkeys . . . don't know anything about directing, cameras, or people."

"Well . . . I'm glad you think I know something." Penny winced inwardly at her callow reply. "Thanks," she added, glancing up into his smiling dark eyes. At five-ten it was rare for any man to look down at her. With Joel, who according to fan magazines was six feet four in his stocking feet, she actually felt like a petite little thing.

"How old are you?" Joel asked bluntly, stepping in front of her and blocking her way.

"Why?" Penny felt the familiar confusion of irritation and helplessness whenever she was confronted by him.

"You're tough to figure." He looked at her hard, and she prayed that Max or someone would summon him to deal with all of the publicity people who had come to meet them.

"Twenty-seven." She met his eyes evenly.

He laughed. "You seem older . . . and younger."

Penny tried to smile. "I guess that's another compliment."

"It is." Joel's dark eyes swept down her body.

Penny's heart was thundering, yet she could do nothing to terminate the awkwardness of the moment. Joel extended his hand, a large, muscular hand with long, sturdy fingers. His thick, curly black hair was sprinkled with gray; prematurely, she thought, for his strong face with the high Indian cheekbones and deep-set eyes had at times an almost boyish quality. Perhaps he was in his mid-thirties.

"Penny, Penny." His eyes sparkled with mirth as he repeated her name. "Why don't we have dinner?"

Penny managed to hide her surprise as she clutched the bag filled with scripts. "That's nice of you but—"

"Oh, you have to work." Joel fixed her with an amused but undeniably sexy look. "You can't work all the time. Not with all of this sea and fresh air and. . . . Have you seen the sea, by the way? I'm about to take my baptismal dip. Why not join me?"

Penny laughed to cover her embarrassment. If only everything he said did not sound as if it were coming from a TV script. If only she hadn't seen just this flirtatious come-on on the monitor back in the New York control room.

"Please." As he took her hand, the sensation was like a fierce pain. She wanted to jerk her hand away. She was too acutely aware of every detail of that hand, its surprisingly smooth palm, the gentleness of a grip that she would have imagined to be harsh.

"La Mer is one of the loveliest restaurants on the northeast coast. I'd say it ranks with some of the best restaurants in France. It's a good place to begin your culinary education."

"What makes you think I'm not already educated . . . culinarily, that is?"

Joel laughed appreciatively at her feisty retort.

"I really can't." Penny hoped her smile was convincingly grateful but firm. She did not want to get off on the wrong foot with him. She had to work with him. It was possible that Max would even assign one of his scenes for her to direct. It was crucial to her professional well-being that their relationship remain on a steady, uncomplicated, even keel.

"Are you one of those never-mix-business-with-pleasure girls?" His dark eyes were moody now, and he reminded her even more of the rapacious Buck Handlin, the character he played on the show.

"I guess." Penny feigned a self-assurance she did not feel. "Maybe some other night." At all costs, she thought, she would avoid that meeting, but for the moment she needed to extricate herself from an increasingly awkward situation.

"Yes." He paused with a tantalizing smile that was brazenly suggestive. "Yes, maybe some other night."

Joel held her eyes, and Penny fought not to turn away as if this struggle between them held great significance. This, Penny thought as his magnetic eyes signaled their intent, was the look that had made him the daytime soap's most famous lover. It was the look of a man who charmed and devoured women with the primitive, reckless ease and grace of a barracuda.

Finally he turned away from her and without a word hurried down the street to join his fellow actors and Max. Penny walked back to the window full of elegant old-fashioned clothing, her cheeks burning. With what? Indignation? Shock?

Damn! Dammit if she wasn't infatuated with him. She rummaged in the canvas bag for her sunglasses and crossed the street to where the technical crew and other nonacting members of the *Dream of Life* team were piling into several vans. She was not some naïve, unaware ninny who had no notion of her own feelings. She was incredibly drawn to him and the knowledge infuriated her because half the women in the United States were in love with him too. She liked to think of herself as unique, as an intelligent, rational woman, and yet. . . . And yet she had succumbed to all of that superficial charm just like millions of other women.

It really made her furious, though no one would have guessed

13

from looking at her almost bland, freckled face that anything could arouse that kind of ire; that she, a perfectly sane, unusually sensible woman from a perfectly average Presbyterian family in Orange, Virginia, could fall for a lady-killer like Joel Sanborne. It annoyed her that she was simply one of a majority who found the daytime soap opera star so irresistible. He was a veritable scoundrel! A liar, a cheat, a man who seduced women with no thought whatsoever of the future. Well, of course she realized he only did those things within the context of the show, but there was something in his behavior that led her to believe that his ability to portray the conniving, ruthless, charming Buck Handlin stemmed from the fact that Buck Handlin and Joel Sanborne were not that dissimilar.

In any case he made her nervous. At the studio she avoided him to the point of darting in doorways when she saw him coming. It was stupid, of course, and she wasn't pleased at her childish response. She just didn't know what else to do.

Now obviously there was no way to avoid Joel while the show was on remote. Their entire group including cameramen, make-up artist, costumer, writer, four actors, technicians, and Max and herself numbered only twenty.

Penny climbed into the van that was reserved for members of the crew. Why had Joel singled her out? The encounter had left her feeling rattled. She took a deep breath in an effort to dispel the speedy feeling their conversation had fostered. She had never really spoken to him before. No doubt he, ever practical and scheming, was trying to line up his romantic interest for the next two weeks. Rather, *sexual* interest, she corrected herself. *Let's not get carried away with romance.* With Buck—rather, she corrected herself again, with Joel Sanborne—sex and power were the real issues. And everyone in television knew that remotes were famous for sexual philandering. Always when people returned from location shoots, the gossip was hot with tales of bed-hopping and the abandon that some people feel when they're away from home and the humdrum of their everyday lives.

Well, thought Penny as she gazed out the window of the van,

14

this opportunity was far too important to her. She watched Joel posing with dark-haired Tippy Malone across the street.

"Smile!" Max crouched in front of the four leading actors and took several shots. Tippy was lounging seductively against Joel as his hand encircled her tiny waist. Rumor had it that they had been lovers many years ago and had never fully broken off although Joel had been married briefly several years earlier. Oh, well.

Penny turned away as Joel helped Tippy into a long black limousine. Joel's *real life* love interest was none of her business. She was going to be very busy. There would be no time to think of Joel Sanborne.

But she could not stop thinking of him. As the van maneuvered along the twisting street she saw Joel, in the sleek cream-colored Porsche he had driven up from New York, cut around one of the corners. As if he knew where he was going, which was his style—the way he always appeared. But something in the way he had looked at her had made her feel special, had made her feel more poignantly alive, more hopeful, more excited. . . .

Fool! Joel Sanborne made *every* woman feel precisely the way he had made her feel. She would be in big trouble if she took anything he said or did seriously.

Faye Barker, a plump, bronze-haired, former burlesque entertainer turned makeup artist, climbed into the van, giving free advice on sun protection to everyone within earshot. Faye was everybody's self-appointed fairy godmother. She listened eagerly to everyone's troubles and just as eagerly passed the information on to anyone who would listen.

"I can't sit in the sun," Penny laughed. "I have to work!"

Faye pointed a chubby finger at Penny. "You should take fifteen minutes today. With your skin you'll be in trouble if you don't go gradual. Pay attention now! You'll be outside on the glaring water during the shoot. You oughta work up. . . . You got almost a week before we film on the boat. You better get some sun . . . gradual."

Penny nodded. Faye's advice was law. If you didn't take it,

15

you didn't say so. "I'll work on the scripts outside in the sun." She was wedged in between Johnny Robello, one of the cameramen, and Serge Moarliski, the shy, bespectacled audio man.

After several wrong turns and much laughter about the truth to the legend that there was no way out of Marblehead because the streets were too twisting and confusing, the van finally bumped onto the road that ran along the harbor. Penny pressed her nose to the window, feeling an explosive excitement at the sight of the sparkling waters which were dotted with white sails. There were a number of large yachts moored farther out in the harbor.

As the van climbed the steep hill that led to the New England Yacht Club, Penny twisted in her seat to look back at the magnificent harbor. No wonder Marblehead had been such a flourishing center of trade prior to the Revolutionary War. The entire village seemed to be built on rock, an absolute bastion overlooking the Atlantic Ocean below. And what better fortification than the craggy, rocky coast!

"We're going to be way off here," Faye lamented. "I hate staying in a place that's way off."

"It's a fifteen-minute walk," Johnny Robello offered.

"I'll kill myself on these hills," cried Faye, and everyone laughed because nothing ever suited Faye until it was over, and then it was *the best.* By the time they were ready to go back to New York, Faye would be extolling the virtues of Marblehead *and* the fifteen-minute walk to town.

Just at the foot of another steep incline the van veered off to the right and began descending down a long, leafy lane back toward the ocean.

"Oh! This is nice!" gasped Faye as an enormous white Victorian mansion came into view.

"Don't mind the walk now, huh, Faye?" Johnny Robello nudged the makeup artist, and again everyone had a good laugh.

There was an air of discreet elegance about the New England Yacht Club, and judging from the few cars that were parked in the circular driveway—Mercedeses, Jaguars, sportscars the

16

names of which Penny did not know—the clientele was also elite. Perhaps Irene had been right. Perhaps the other guests would all have blue blood.

Penny smiled to herself as she climbed out of the functional van and mounted the steps to the wide verandalike porch that wrapped around the mansion. Somehow she had imagined they would be staying in a more modest motel, something basic, a place to simply throw one's self into bed after a long day of shooting. The name New England Yacht Club had conjured up some casual establishment on the water with perhaps a tacky marina attached to the grounds. In fact the Yacht Club with its vast, wooded grounds, swimming pool, gardens, and numerous cottages was unquestionably the most luxurious place Penny had ever seen.

While the others went inside to register Penny wandered around the porch till she was overlooking the ocean. The vista from this vantage point was breathtaking. Already she could feel the tension from city life draining out of her. Perhaps Faye was right. Perhaps it would be a wise idea to expose her very pale body to the sun for a fifteen-minute period. Below her, at the edge of the velvety green lawn, was a sign indicating a path that led down to the water's edge. Perhaps she would put on her swimming suit and sit by the ocean while she worked on her scripts. There was no law against mixing a little bit of pleasure with business.

As she turned to go inside she heard Tippy Malone's light, contagious laugh and knew that the first-class limousine crowd had arrived. No doubt Joel Sanborne had arrived before anyone since he was driving his own car and *always* knew his way around. Not wanting to encounter Joel, she settled herself into a large white wicker armchair with cheery green and white cushions. Without really deciding to, she began to work on the scripts. After a while the chatter of recently arrived guests faded, and she was left in the cool silence of the early afternoon. No doubt everyone else was taking the sun; consequently the porch and the surrounding verdant grounds were hushed. Penny

17

worked peacefully with a relaxed, contented smile on her face. With the cool sea breeze ruffling her sandy hair and her sandals kicked to one side, she was able to accomplish five hours' work in less than two.

Around four she stood up, stretched, and with an enormous sense of accomplishment went inside to register. She was told her luggage had already been delivered to her quarters, which were located in one of the several cottages tucked away in secluded, woodsy areas. Key in hand and with a pleasant late-afternoon drowsiness about to overtake her, Penny walked through the fragrant rose garden, past the swimming pool, and into a moist, shaded pine grove where the desk clerk had directed her. She stopped suddenly; her legs felt wobbly and her heart was racing wildly. Joel Sanborne, clad in a very brief navy swimsuit with a towel tossed over one shoulder, was letting himself into his room. Penny checked the number on her own key. His room was next to hers.

She waited until he had disappeared inside his room, then she let herself into her own room. Once inside she was certain there had been a mistake. Surely this room had been meant for Tippy or one of the other stars of *Dream of Life.* In the center of the room there was a large four-poster bed with a lacy coverlet. The bed was so high that it required a small stool to climb into it. Two delicate Sheraton chairs sat on either side of a round cherry table that was placed to the side of a small fireplace, useful should the nights turn cool. Across from this attractive dining area were French doors that opened out onto a small terrace overlooking the ocean.

Penny stared at her luggage, which included her portable typewriter and several boxes of scripts. She was in the right room. She began to unpack quickly. The idea of Joel's presence on the other side of the wall made her nervous, and she undressed with unfamiliar, rapid movements, tossing her wilted travel clothes into a heap in the bottom of a small, primitive armoire.

It was too late for a swim. She was really too tired after all of that work. She stood indecisively in the middle of the room and after a moment found herself standing under a steaming shower. She would be a fool to give up a great room like this just because her imagination was getting the better of her . . . just because she kept thinking that Joel was watching her every move. How dumb! How childish!

Emerging from the shower, Penny slipped into a thin blue cotton robe and pulled the sash tight around her slender waist. Her cheeks were glowing, and with her sandy hair damp and slicked back from her face she had an ingenuous, elfin look. She padded out onto the little terrace in her bare feet. A low haze was forming over the ocean, and the light was soft and diffused. She moved to the little white wrought-iron table and chairs which were situated at the far corner of the terrace. After a moment she sat, legs together, back stiff and straight against the spindly back of the chair. A vine-covered trellis separated her terrace from the terraces on either side. Penny sat very still, certain that Joel was on the other side, almost feeling his breath on her neck. Under the thin blue robe her body prickled.

"You're there?" Joel's voice was low but distinct.

Penny swallowed. She had almost stopped breathing. She waited for someone to reply to his inquiry.

"You are there, aren't you? You smell nice. Can I tempt you over with some awfully nice champagne?"

Her mouth felt parched. She couldn't believe he was speaking to her. What if she answered and then found out he was talking to someone else? She'd feel like a dope!

"I saw you working away up at the main house . . . out on the porch. You can't use work as an excuse. You were up there all afternoon."

Penny opened her mouth and closed it. There was no doubt. He knew she was there.

"Penny . . . ?" His voice sent a warm ripple into the pit of her stomach. He knew she was in the room next to his. He was waiting. She hesitated. She could pretend she hadn't heard. He

19

had no way of knowing she was actually sitting less than four feet from him. He couldn't see through the leafy trellis, could he?

Damn him! He had arranged it. She had been right. He had manipulated her into this room because he was interested in setting up a little "arrangement" for the next two weeks. Her cheeks were stinging with fury as she crept back inside her room.

She was not going to let Joel Sanborne dictate anything to her. She would keep the room and deal with him as a professional. He would respect her . . . as a director. That was the only thing that mattered. Penny pulled the pillow over her head and through an act of sheer determination managed to fall into a damp, exhausted slumber.

But in her dreams that determination wavered, and her imagination, free from the restrictions imposed by her waking self, arranged for Joel to discover her, alone, in the control room back in the New York studio. In the dream Penny was watching a replay of the day's taping on one of the small monitors when he called to her.

"Penny . . ." There was a click as the control room door closed behind him, and even before she swiveled around in her chair to face him she felt his presence. It was as if a seductively tropical breeze had swept into the room, and she sucked in her breath to savor its heady fragrance.

"Everyone's gone . . ." Joel towered over her as she turned her back on the monitor and gazed up into his dark, brooding eyes. The audio from the monitor became muted as Penny's concentration was drawn to his lanky form—the snug, faded jeans which strained over his hips and thighs, the familiar red plaid flannel shirt, also worn and faded.

Penny met his eyes boldly, a knowing smile playing on her parted lips as he moved closer until his knees were pressing into hers. She did not flinch as his hand moved slowly to encircle her neck. The power of his dark eyes was dizzying but Penny did not turn away, and as he placed his hand firmly behind her neck, she allowed the warm pressure of his fingers to propel her to her feet.

She took a deep, steadying breath as her body came into full contact with his hard, muscular form.

Her breasts seemed to expand as they brushed lightly against his taut chest. She felt the suppleness of her own body as it yearned toward his. She wanted desperately for him to touch her, to feel his hands driving her further and further into him. But he made no move; only his dark eyes pierced into her. They seemed to penetrate into her very soul.

"I want you . . ." he rasped, and she gasped then as he pressed into her until every nuance of his manliness seemed to sear through her thin denim jeans.

His face wore the hungry, intense look of Buck Handlin, the look that thrilled his fans. "I want you now!"

"Yes!" Penny cried with unabashed eagerness.

Joel's mouth was hard and demanding, but she met the fervid thrusts of his tongue with a hunger equal to his. As he furiously sought to explore every crevice of those moist recesses, Penny groaned with pleasure, wrapping her arms around his throbbing body and drawing him closer, ever closer. She could not have him close enough, and she twisted and writhed to exhort more and more pleasure from his steely form.

The kiss stormed on and on, as turbulent but somehow as right, as natural, and as ordained as a gale at sea. The violence of their desire was awesome, yet because it surged equally through them both it seemed to Penny almost like some religious ecstasy . . . a battle of purity. The flaming purity of the flesh.

Finally she could stand it no longer. She pulled away from him, drenched with longing and wanting more. He did not need prodding. His hands moved swiftly to the buttons of her blouse and slipped the confining fabric from her trembling shoulders.

When she felt those large hands slide along the silken curves of her breasts, she threw her head back, murmuring his name over and over. And when his tongue teased the rosy tips, she felt her body convulse and shudder as ecstatic waves of pleasure shook her.

"Make love to me, Joel," she groaned as she grasped his thick

21

dark hair, pulling him closer to her waiting softness. The pleasure was so intense that she staggered. "Joel . . . Joel . . . now!"

Penny woke with a start at the sound of her own voice. She was drenched with perspiration, her body tingling. Had that ever happened before? Her body was alive . . . something *real* had happened to her!

But it was only a dream. She blinked twice and swallowed hard to try to make some sense out of what had happened to her. She had felt his mouth moving toward. . . . She gasped and drew her knees up against her chest to stop the pounding of her heart. The bed was strange, the room was strange, and her breath was still coming in staccato pants. She could not seem to focus, and when a knock sounded at the door she pulled her robe on over her naked body and stumbled across the room to answer it.

She blinked groggily into Joel Sanborne's startled face, still uncertain if she was awake or dreaming. It was several seconds before she realized that the thin robe had parted to fully reveal one well-rounded breast with its hard pink nipple. She flushed, then quickly pulled the robe shut, explaining unnecessarily that she had been asleep.

"I thought you might have changed your mind about dinner." Joel stepped inside the room but did not close the door.

Penny glanced wildly around for her travel clock. She felt totally disoriented.

"You worked too hard. All afternoon while the rest of us were playing." Joel observed her with a little smile. "You need a good supper and then a full night's sleep. You'll be fine tomorrow."

"I certainly don't feel like I can edit any more scripts today." Penny backed away from him and ran her hand through her hair. Did he know how she felt? What if she had cried out his name in that dream? What if he had heard her moaning, and what if he knew that she had just been on the point of making love with him . . . in the dream, that is.

"Get dressed," he ordered, then laughed at the alarmed look on her face. "I'll wait in my room. You have to eat."

22

Penny smiled at her foolishness. "All right," she said. "Dinner —but you're not taking me or anything like that. Okay?"

A smiled played around Joel's mouth as he regarded her. "Okay," he said finally, and he turned and left.

"What am I doing?" Penny asked her incredulous face as she smoothed a light cream into her skin. "What am I doing going to dinner with Joel Sanborne? I must be nuts. I must be!"

Twenty minutes later Penny tapped at the door of Joel's room. She was dressed in crisp gray linen slacks, a white blouse, and was carrying a white linen jacket. She had purposefully passed over any clothes that might have signaled anything other than an "I'm-here-for-business" statement, and as if to underscore her intent she had made a point of wearing her glasses, which she generally only wore for work.

"Come in," he called, and his voice sounded irritated. He gestured for Penny to sit down, then he retreated to the far side of the room to conclude his telephone conversation. He scowled and nodded impatiently at the person on the other end of the line.

"I did not say. . . . Dammit, you've blown the whole thing out of proportion. I don't know how you got this number. I've tried to be decent about it, but really . . . you're going too far!"

Penny sat tensely on the edge of the chair trying to look as though she wasn't listening, which would have been impossible.

"Don't call again," Joel whispered tightly, and as he hung up he grimaced. "Sorry," he said, looking at Penny.

Penny nodded awkwardly, wishing she had never agreed to go to dinner with him. The phone conversation had sent her imagination spinning. No doubt the call had been from a woman, some rejected lover, probably, who had desperately tracked him down. She flinched as he took her elbow and guided her out the door. There really seemed to be no way out of it.

"That," he said after a few minutes, "was an hysterical woman. Would you believe . . . a fan that I once invited to see a taping at the studio?"

"That's terrible," Penny replied, but she was leery of the explanation, and her entire sympathy was with the woman.

"You don't believe me." Joel sensed her dubiousness.

"Of course I believe you," Penny affirmed, not wanting to alienate him and thinking again what a stupid mistake it had been to agree to have dinner with him.

"Well, it's true enough." Joel shook his head in disgust. "I had my New York number changed twice. First to an unlisted number and then this woman managed, God knows how, to get my unlisted number. She calls at all hours. It's sad, I know, but after a while my . . . compassion dries up."

Penny glanced at him with a new flicker of interest. He did seem to be telling the truth. "I guess it's hard being a star."

Joel snorted derisively. "Hardly a star, Penny. A soap opera actor is hardly a star. I don't delude myself about that!"

Again Joel's response shocked her. Somehow she had imagined his success in daytime television would have blown his ego out of all proportion. Yet here he was almost putting himself down.

They walked down the winding hill that led to a little footpath which ran along the ocean's edge.

"Do me a favor." Joel's dark eyes studied her intently. "Don't talk about the business. Let's just pretend we're normal people."

The garden of La Mer was brimming with sophisticated clientele. In the darkness candles illuminated white tablecloths, and a young man seated on a stone bench under a gnarled olive tree played Bach on his classical guitar.

"Madame." The maître d' held the chair for Penny.

"A bottle of champagne," Joel ordered in French, and the French maître d' responded with a grateful smile. "Whatever you suggest. I leave it to you."

"*Oui, monsieur.*" The maître d' bowed his approval and disappeared.

"That was nice of you," Penny observed with a surprised smile.

"What?" Joel responded curiously.

"Speaking to the maître d' in his own language. Obviously he loved you for it. He probably dies to speak his native tongue."

Joel gave a curt laugh. "Selfish," he said. "On my part. I like to use my French. I don't get that much opportunity. Some people think I'm just affected."

"Well, I thought it was nice," Penny repeated, and this time he seemed to accept the compliment more easily. She looked around as waiters swished past carrying culinary masterpieces, setting up silver wine buckets, popping corks, bowing and whispering.

"What a lovely spot." Penny's eyes were bright with excitement.

"And you were going to stay in your room and dine on bread and water . . . working until dawn." Joel studied her with an amused expression.

Penny laughed. "You're right. But I was nervous about all the work."

"It's bad to work on an empty stomach," Joel observed as the waiter showed him the bottle of champagne. "Yes, that will be just fine." Again Joel addressed the waiter in French.

"Where did you learn such perfect French? At least I think it's perfect," Penny added.

"In college," Joel answered. "I was an exchange student . . . about a million years ago, but I've kept up with my French. Have you been? To France that is?"

Penny shook her head. "But I'd like to."

"You'd love it!" Joel leaned forward with a kind of ingenuous intensity Penny had never seen from him before. As he spoke of his student years in France and his love of the French countryside his expression was rapt, his dark eyes flashing with almost childlike enthusiasm.

"Here's to France!" Joel raised his glass in a toast, and Penny touched her glass to his. "Maybe we'll go, you and I."

"Of course we will." Penny felt her cheeks color.

"You never know," Joel said with sparkling eyes, and despite her flush of embarrassment Penny laughed.

25

He was nice. The realization stunned her. For the first time since she had been hired by *Dream of Life* over three years ago, she was not thinking of him as the villainous Buck Handlin. She sipped the champagne, feeling her body melt into a sublime state of relaxation as she listened to Joel speak of his last trip to France.

"That's why I love La Mer." Joel gestured broadly to their romantic surroundings. "It's French in the best sense . . . that is, it's not phony, but it is elegant and the quality of the cuisine couldn't be better. The chef here used to have a wonderful restaurant in Cannes. That's how I heard of this spot. I've driven from New York all the way to Marblehead for dinner."

"I never would have guessed." Penny's smile was easy. She felt as if they were old friends, as if they dined this way often.

"Madame?" The waiter's assumption about her marital status brought a new blush of color to her cheeks. *"Mademoiselle,"* she corrected him with a humorous glint in her eyes.

"For openers"—Penny felt a tingle of nervous excitement as she tested her French—"for openers I will have Coquilles St. Jacques and then something light . . . I believe the salmon with fresh tarragon and *la salade après, s'il vous plait."*

She glanced slyly at Joel, whose mouth had flown open in astonishment. He chuckled as he gave the waiter his order and then he laughed heartily. "I assure you I will never make any more assumptions about you, Penny Phillips. But now tell me . . . how does a young woman named Penny Phillips come to speak such excellent French and know so much about food *and* stay so thin?"

"I don't eat the food," Penny confessed. "I just read about it. I've never tasted most of the things I read about, but I subscribe to all of those luscious-looking food magazines. I read cookbooks before I go to sleep at night instead of mysteries."

Joel was shaking his head with an intrigued smile. "How bizarre." He laughed and patted her hand in a casual gesture that nevertheless managed to raise small bumps of intense pleasure all along her arm.

The meal was absolute perfection, and with the melodious guitar in the background they dined as easily as if they had been traveling together and enjoying French cuisine for years.

When they left the lush Roman garden Joel slipped his arm easily through hers, and they started back to the Yacht Club chattering on about their meal and laughing, because although they were both stuffed they were already looking forward to the next repast.

Finally they fell silent. With a warm wind blowing up from the sea Penny felt a tug at her stomach, a yearning of such intensity she thought she would cry out. What was happening? It was as if Joel Sanborne had unlocked all of the most intense and profound cravings of her body. Back in New York she was dating several men but had made it a point to keep her involvements casual, uncomplicated. With her career foremost in her mind she was not willing to invest the time or emotional energy that any serious relationship would require. But the rhythm of their steps, the sensation of his muscular forearm, Joel's almost overpowering presence had unleashed a fierce need that surpassed anything she had ever felt.

As they entered the grounds his arm slipped expertly around her waist, and when he paused to lean against a tree the conflict she experienced made her positively dizzy.

"What a night." He smiled lazily and raised his eyes to the shimmering stars. She was so acutely aware of his lean, sinewy body that her mind was a blank. All conversation dried up as an insistent pulsing in her stomach played havoc with her sense of reality. She could feel the heat of his body through his jacket. She glanced sideways at his stern, magnificent profile, relieved to see that he was still smiling, that he was relaxed and seemed to have no knowledge of the uncontrollable sensations he set off in her. Thank God he didn't feel the same way. She wondered if she would have the power to resist his passion. A wave of anxiety swept over her. This man was too dynamic, too single-minded and egotistical; if she let him he could dominate her life.

Good God . . . what if he had overheard her calling his name

27

earlier in the evening? She was mortified by the idea, but even her mortification did not subdue those insistent little flames that licked and teased inside her body. She still felt possessed by the man.

She swallowed hard and tried desperately to think of a congenial ending for an evening that had, surprisingly enough, been perfect. It was late. She really should go in. She took a deep breath to steady herself and gazed up at the stars with a bleak, worried expression.

"Nice, huh?" Joel slid his arm around her waist and drew her against the side of his body. Her heart seemed to stop. But she could not move away from him and felt her slender, soft curves conforming to his muscular form.

Now she felt a current of desire emanating from his body. No, she must have imagined it. He was still smiling up at the stars. But his hand was playing idly around her midsection, his fingers testing the firmness of her tiny waist, spreading, smoothing, and caressing.

"I have an early call tomorrow," Penny said faintly.

Joel smiled down at her, and there was an unmistakable gleam in his eye.

"One more minute." Joel shifted slightly until she felt his thigh rubbing gently against hers. His hand, still roaming around her waist, burned into her.

The sensation of his hard thigh pressed against hers unnerved her, and she shifted casually as if she had not realized his intention. What on earth was she doing and why wasn't she going inside?

His hand moved up her back creating a hot wave of pleasure along her spine. "Very straight," he complimented her with a teasing, easy smile. "Not everyone has a straight back, you know." He pressed his fingers into her vertebrae with the expertise of a masseur.

"No tension here." Joel massaged her back, his hand dangerously near the gentle curve of her breast.

"I should . . ." She broke off as he turned her toward him, his

28

hands resting on her shoulders. She stared at him blankly, overcome by the conflicting feelings that were surging inside of her. Hadn't they stood just like this in her dream? Just touching . . . barely touching their two bodies?

Joel's eyes glistened as he smiled at her. He was going to kiss her. She prepared herself for the onslaught.

But there was no way she could have been ready for the tenderness of his warm, soft mouth as he pressed his lips against hers. The shock of his infinite gentleness sent new waves of desire coursing through her body, and she swayed into him, parting her lips to signal him her acquiescence. His mouth widened slowly. He was in no hurry. Only Penny felt an almost uncontrollable urge to put her arms around his powerful body as she had done in the dream and melt into him.

Impetuously she flicked the tip of her tongue against his lips. He responded with unbridled passion to her invitation, pressing her against his body until she felt his arousal in her very core. Dimly it occurred to her that *this* was the very moment she had feared, but now that it was happening, just as in the dream, she wanted more.

When he pulled away to stare at her she felt herself straining toward him. There was a touch of awe in his face as he studied her. He was breathing heavily, trying to control his passion. She saw that he was uncertain, but she was in no position to help. She wanted him . . . wanted him more than she had ever wanted anyone, more than she had ever dreamed was possible.

He moved back to her and deftly removed her glasses, sliding them easily into his jacket pocket as if he were accustomed to the movement.

"You're a very beautiful woman." His voice was husky with desire, and Penny felt a ripple of pleasure at having aroused this dynamic man to such heights.

She came to him eagerly, and the ease with which he opened her mouth and slipped his tongue inside made her gasp with an insatiable hunger. It excited her that he knew precisely what he was doing. The innuendo of his slow, deep stroking tongue was too much to bear. She flung her arms around him with an urgency that she realized was totally new to her. She felt an unaccustomed, brazen ruthlessness, and when he groaned his pleasure a new sort of ecstasy burst in on her heart.

How she wanted to please this man! It was the idea of pleasing him, of eliciting from him those marvelous sounds that drove her on. Her tongue was fire inside of his mouth; her hands were daring as they explored the brawny muscles of his shoulders.

She felt him guiding her to one of the little wrought-iron benches that were strategically placed on the grounds. His hands seemed to know her body. He spread them, fanlike, over her hips and molded her more firmly against him, kneading and directing her in a rhythmic rocking motion.

As they sank onto the bench his hand glided over her breast.

"I have to go . . ." Penny tried to shift away from his pursuing hand, but it hovered over her breasts like a magnet until she felt herself arching toward it, eager to feel the pressure of his fingers against her hardened nipples.

"I know you do." Joel stroked her ample breast with a reverent expression. He pressed his fingers firmly into her nipple, then gathered both breasts in his two hands and stared into her eyes.

For an instant she thought she was going to swoon. The sensation of his hands on her breasts coupled with the impassioned, glazed look in his eyes made her head spin.

"I've wanted to do this all evening." He bent his head down and buried it in her breasts, nuzzling against her.

"I really do have to go," Penny pleaded as she felt his hot mouth brush against her bare skin. Irrationally she pictured herself tearing off the blouse, the bra which separated her from the full impact of the sensations they both desired.

"Yes, I know you do." Joel forced himself to an upright position. His eyes scanned her face again hungrily, as if he could not stop looking at her, as if he were memorizing every feature.

"We do have an early day tomorrow, don't we?" His hand strayed back to her breast and cupped it gently.

Penny nodded.

"We don't seem to be going anywhere, though." Joel smiled languidly. His slightest gesture, she thought, was like an eloquent seduction. He didn't even have to do anything and he still radiated sensuality.

He looked down at his hand, which was idly tracing the perimeter of her breast. He looked back at her with a crooked smile.

"I have your glasses in my pocket." He seemed amused.

"I know." Penny said and smiled back uncertainly.

"I guess we should go in." He continued to drink in her features. "Separately, of course."

Penny did not answer. He seemed to be teasing her, and with a stab of insecurity she wondered how he had been able to turn off all that passion so quickly, so effectively.

"I want to make love to you . . ." His pronouncement took her completely by surprise, for his expression had given no indication of his feelings. Suddenly she was deep in his arms, and once again they were kissing with the same ravenous intensity. The sky seemed to be opening for her, and she felt it was the same for him. Simultaneously they drew back to catch a breath, then plunged back together to simulate that quintessential act that it was clear they both desired.

"Really!" Penny forced herself to twist out of his ironlike embrace. "I'll be out of it tomorrow . . . if I . . . don't . . ."

Joel closed his eyes in consent, and with a supreme act of will shook his powerful body as if to dispel the impact of their kisses. His teasing manner was gone when he looked at her, and when she stood up he seemed to be struggling with himself.

"Okay." He laced his fingers through hers as he dragged himself to his feet. "I'll let you go tonight. But I won't give up so easily next time."

Penny cast him a dubious glance, but he had regained his composure and only regarded her with a naughty, roguish smile.

"And don't pretend you'll want me to give up." Joel swung her arm blithely as if they were two schoolchildren. "You have given yourself away."

31

Penny smiled in spite of herself. His teasing held no threat. "We'll see." She accepted her glasses and shoved them back up on her nose.

"Is that a pun?" Joel tilted her chin up to his face.

"I didn't intend it to be." Penny felt another onslaught of desire surging at the gates. She wanted to get inside her room, fast.

"In fact," Joel said pointedly, "I promise you *not* to give up easily at all. In fact . . . I promise . . ." As Penny reached for the key to her room he drew her to him in one last, searing kiss before bidding her good night.

## CHAPTER TWO

"This dialogue is lousy!" Max fumed under his breath. "Penny! We gotta do something about this!"

Penny closed the notebook where she was recording camera shots and ran over to Max's side. No doubt he had another errand for her to run. Since they had begun shooting two days ago she had done nothing even remotely creative. Max, who was usually ultrasensitive about using his ADs as gofers, had kept her on the run day and night. Most of the time she had not even been around for the filming.

"Phone New York." Max ran his hand through his thinning hair. "Damn! We're going to lose more time, but this dialogue stinks. Joel has come up with something that at least makes sense." He shoved some papers at Penny. "Read it and see if you can convince someone at the agency."

Penny nodded obediently and set off to find a telephone.

"And hurry!" Max cried after her.

Right, hurry. She had done nothing but hurry. Between trips to the coast guard to secure permission to film off Devil Island, a broken camera lens, constant script problems, and Tippy's temperament, she had not had time to exchange more than a few words with Joel. By the time she finished taking notes from Max after each day's shoot, Joel was already asleep in order to be up at five or six the next morning.

As Penny ran through the twisting Marblehead streets she glanced back over her shoulder at the scene in progress. Archie Marshall, who played the "good guy," was arguing with Joel, who in the character of Buck Handlin was limping around with one foot in a cast. They had been shooting exteriors outside an old Georgian mansion since dawn, and so far nothing had gone right. Penny smiled wearily. So much for all of those racy tales about remotes. So far no one had had time to do anything but work. For the past two evenings dinner had consisted of soggy tuna fish sandwiches and lukewarm Folonari wine.

Penny located a phone booth outside a little market and dug into the pocket of her khaki jacket for change. She had begun referring to the little phone booth as her office since here was where she spent most of her time. How nice it would be to wander the streets of Marblehead like the other tourists, to sip lemonade in the shade, or just to sit and people-watch.

"Hello . . . hello?" Finally the call went through, and after several wrong connections at the agency Penny began to tactfully suggest script changes to the New York advertising executive whose approval she needed. She did not mention that one of the actors (Joel to be precise) had made the changes, because this particular executive resented any "intellectual" interference from his cast members. And naturally she did not use Max's colorful vocabulary in describing the inadequacies of the script. Somehow, though it amazed her that the executive had not seen how ridiculous her reasoning was, she managed to acquire the necessary approval for the script change by saying that the dialogue was "not suitable with the physical terrain of the location." Her explanation was apparently oblique enough to satisfy the corporate mind.

When it came right down to it, Penny thought as she trudged back up the street to the location, the executive did not really care what the dialogue was as long as he was consulted and his authority remained intact.

"Hey there!" Archie Marshall, as blond and blue-eyed as Joel was dark and swarthy, was striding toward her.

"What are you doing?" Penny looked beyond Archie to where Max was waving his arms frantically at one of the cameramen.

"Goin' home," Archie said with a grin.

"What happened now?" Penny grimaced.

"The light's bad." Archie looked triumphant. "How about a drink, Pen? The Landmark Tavern makes a mean Bloody Mary."

"The light's bad?" Penny repeated shaking her head. "When are we going to get any film? We're so far behind already."

"Well, you know Max." Archie rolled his eyes in a derogatory manner, and Penny bit back a staunch defense of her boss. Maybe Max wasn't the most original director in the business but he was certainly one of the kindest, and as far as Penny was concerned kindness in television went a long way. She had never heard Max utter a demeaning word to any of his actors . . . least of all Archer Marshall. This constant berating of Max was the one unpleasant characteristic of Archie's—Archie was usually highly respected for his kindness, his even temper, and his ability to successfully balance his television career and his family life.

"Thanks anyway, Archie. I have to check in with Max." Penny started up the incline, but Archie took hold of her arm.

"You need a break, kid. I think Max is taking advantage of you. There are rules, you know. That's why we have unions."

"He's not, really." Penny smiled. "He's just Max, and I don't mind."

"Seems more frazzled than usual," Archie commented drily, but as Max approached his attitude changed. He greeted the harried director with an amicable slap on the back.

"So?" Max questioned Penny through his smeared glasses.

"It's okay," she said. "From now on let me handle him. I think I have the key."

"Take the day off. See you tomorrow morning, my room at

35

eight sharp." Max smiled weakly at Archie. "Good scene, Arch."

"Take it easy, old boy," Archie called after Max, then turning back to Penny he winked. "I say you and I drive down the coast for a twilight dip. Then maybe a couple of good martinis and who knows . . ."

Penny stared at him. There was nothing subtle in his invitation, and its suggestiveness had taken her aback. She removed her glasses and began to clean them on her shirt sleeve. Archie had had her to his house three times for dinner. She knew his wife and their two daughters, knew them well.

"Come on . . . a little swim." Archie gave her his most winning boyish grin.

So this was Archer Marshall, staunch family man, on remote. "Thanks, Archie, but I promised Irene we'd drive to Salem the first chance we had." Penny threw him a brisk smile as she began trudging back up to where the rest of the crew and hopefully Joel were still packing it in for the day. So much for the straight and narrow Archer Marshall. God, if you couldn't believe in the Archer Marshalls of the world, who could you believe in?

By the time she reached the old Georgian mansion where they had been shooting, everyone except Johnny Robello and his assistant had gone. Penny sat on the sagging steps and gazed out toward the ocean. In the late afternoon light the seagulls dipped and swooped.

She felt as if her evening with Joel had happened weeks ago or that perhaps it had only been a dream. Odd, how distorted one's sense of time was when you were in a strange, new place, working ridiculous hours. Penny sighed. She had been so afraid of Joel, yes . . . really afraid of him, but now that she had her first minute's respite, all she could think of was being with him. But she shouldn't get her hopes up. Probably he had plans by now. He and Tippy had publicity obligations; it was probably foolish to think he had an evening free.

She pulled herself to her feet, brushed off her jeans, and meandered back into the center of the village feeling lethargic and melancholy. Archie had already latched on to Irene and was bending her ear at a small table in the café. Most of the day tourists had deserted the square. It was stupid to wander around being depressed on her first free night in days.

But back in her room she could not summon up any enthusiasm, and that annoyed her. She heard Joel enter his room, and her pulse quickened as she waited for her phone to ring.

Dammit if living next door to him didn't make things awkward. She had no right to expect anything from him—maybe she should change rooms so she wouldn't be so damned aware of his presence.

She froze when she heard someone knock at his door. A few minutes later she heard a woman sobbing. She recognized the sobs immediately. They belonged to Tippy Malone.

Penny paced around the room several times, then throwing off her jeans and shirt, stepped under a steaming shower. Tippy had a right to be there. Tippy had a right to cry. Joel had a right to do anything he wanted to do.

But she felt sick with disappointment, and she knew that she would have to take some firm, immediate action in order to dispel a crippling depression. As she put on fresh makeup she forced her mind to deal logically with the situation. She would (a) change her room and (b) buy an advanced French grammar book to improve her French; she would then (c) call Irene or Faye or anyone and drive to neighboring Salem for a sumptuous fish dinner with lots of wine!

When the phone rang she flew to answer it.

"Your place or mine?" It was Joel, and the sound of his deep baritone made her skin prickle with desire. "Do you know a good place for lobster?" she asked breathlessly. "I have food on my mind."

"And I"—Joel gave a delicious low laugh—"have something else on mine."

"Maybe a compromise?" Penny could not believe how the mere sound of his voice made her heart pound.

37

"I heard your shower . . . I confess to an erotic response. You looked fabulous in those jeans. Are you still there?"

"I'm here." Penny laughed and wondered why she wasn't annoyed when he was at the moment behaving exactly like the wretched Buck Handlin. "Yes, Buck . . . I'm here."

"Touché." Joel laughed. "I'll give you ten minutes to do whatever you have to do. And no argument . . . I'm buying you dinner. Best lobster this side of Maine is a joint I know in Gloucester. Not fancy, but good. Gloucester's about an hour from here. If I can find my way out of Marblehead we should be there before dark. Are you a swimmer?"

"Red Cross junior when I was sixteen," Penny announced exuberantly.

"So bring along your suit and after we stuff ourselves on lobster and waddle around Gloucester we'll go for a moonlight dip. Does that sound good?"

Did it sound good?!! Penny replaced the receiver and reminded herself not to let out a telltale yelp of excitement. She put on her well-worn green and white bikini and over it a pair of white duck pants and a peach-colored cotton sweater. She was about to put on her contact lenses but thought that was going a bit too far. Anyway, she couldn't swim in soft lenses, and she had left her hard lenses back in New York.

She stopped abruptly and stared at her flushed face in the bathroom mirror. Was she really prepared for this? Did she really think she could handle a man like Joel Sanborne?


"Twenty-seven, huh?" Joel regarded Penny wryly as they left the Land's End Tavern and walked out onto the deserted Gloucester streets.

"I know." Penny glanced at him. "You're not sure if I seem older or younger than twenty-seven."

"Nope." Joel stroked his chin thoughtfully. "I've decided. You seem older but you look younger . . . which, as far as I'm concerned, makes you just about perfect."

"And you?" Penny asked.

38

"Too old to be playing games in front of a camera." Joel's eyes clouded, and she felt him tense up. "I'm thirty-six."

"Why do you say playing games? You're terribly successful . . . one of the all-time most popular daytime actors. And you're good."

"Well, thanks." Joel's reply was cynical.

"I mean . . ." Penny stammered.

"I know," Joel interjected. "But how would you know I'm a good actor? All I do is play mean old Buck Handlin . . . rape and pillage and smile and lie."

"You must be doing something right." Penny felt herself in the strange position of reassuring him. Yes, it was almost as if he needed reassurance. "I don't think your fans love you just because you're a scoundrel. I mean that would imply there were an awful lot of self-destructive women . . . and men out there. I think they see something else in Buck."

Penny broke off abruptly. She had never thought of it that way before, but it was true. People responded to the confusion in Buck, not the evil streak.

"Oh, I don't know," Joel mused. "I'm getting a little fed up with being a male sex object."

Again Penny was astounded by his perception of himself. All along she had just assumed that he reveled in his matinee idol role. She felt as if she were meeting Joel Sanborne for the first time.

"Funny," she said after a moment. "I never thought about *male* sex objects."

Joel jabbed her playfully in the ribs. "You see how much I can teach you?"

They walked around the village of Gloucester chatting easily about the day's shoot, discussing tomorrow's script, and agreeing that location work was much more fun than being stuck all day in the New York studio. As they walked Joel slipped his arm around her waist and pulled her against him until his face brushed against her hair.

Penny felt her limbs weaken, and her body seemed to melt into his, her gait corresponding so perfectly to his as they walked. There was a sliver of a moon and an unusually warm breeze.

"If it's this warm up here," he commented, "imagine what they're going through in New York City. I think it hit a hundred and three today."

"Lucky us to be on remote," Penny said, then sighed.

"A perfect night for a swim," Joel whispered, and his breath was warm, smelling faintly of the white wine they had had with the lobster.

Penny averted her eyes from the intensity of his gaze. The back of her neck prickled, and she was painfully aware that his breathing had accelerated, that he was as affected as she was by the closeness of their bodies. Beneath her casual summer attire her bikini felt warm and damp. She had been hoping he would not mention the swim, but it was clear that he had his mind set on it. As they passed his Porsche he darted over and rummaged inside the trunk for two large beach towels. Back beside her he pointed enthusiastically to the beach below, then grabbing her hand he helped her over the huge rocks and down onto the pebbly beach below. She considered lying, saying that she had not worn her swimming suit, but somehow she felt he already knew better. Under the white slacks her green and white bikini felt skimpier and more inadequate than ever.

"What a night!" Joel threw his arms wide in an ecstatic gesture, then turned to her with a nonchalant grin as he unzipped his white trousers.

"Very . . . rocky." Penny cringed at the stupidity of her observation, or rather at the desperate tone that had crept into her voice. Suddenly nervous, she turned her back as he removed his pants. The beach, which was on the outskirts of Gloucester, seemed to stretch endlessly in either direction. Like most all of the beaches in the vicinity it was covered with rocks of varying sizes—large boulders near the road, then medium-sized rocks—but near the surf were sort of small, pebbly rocks interspersed with a few enormous, prehistoric-looking slabs which would be nice for sunbathing during the day. There was no sand whatever.

"Rocks can be comfortable," said Joel, who was proving his point by lying prone, face up to the starry night, on one of the large slabs.

"You don't look very comfortable," Penny remarked, but the light, casual laugh stuck in her throat.

"I am." Joel turned to her, his dark eyes dancing. He seemed to find her obvious discomfort amusing. Penny stood awkwardly, still clothed but feeling somehow totally vulnerable, as if she were standing naked before him. He rolled off the large monolith and approached her slowly.

"Aren't you going to swim?" he inquired darkly. "You're in good hands, you know."

"I'm sure I am." Penny smiled uncertainly then glanced longingly at the surf which was breaking close to the rocky beach.

"You're looking at a former lifeguard." Joel guided her chin with one hand, forcing her to look into his eyes. "I'll help."

Gingerly he removed her glasses, then slowly his hands moved to the bottom of her sweater and he began to lift it up, his eyes never waivering from hers. She knew there was something she should be saying, but her mind was a complete blank. He paused as his hand lightly grazed her breast, then he removed his hands from the peach sweater and stepped back from her. He placed his two hands on either side of her head and studied her with a grim, melancholy expression.

"I'm going in the water," he announced, then he turned abruptly and left her staring after his retreating figure. Penny looked away. His navy trunks were brief; like a second skin they revealed every nuance of his strong, manly form. Yes, all six feet four of his body was perfect, the muscles as smooth and well-defined as a Michelangelo sculpture. His legs, which were long and quite muscular, were sparsely covered with dark hair. She turned back to the ocean just in time to see him splashing out to sea. He dived and disappeared under a wave.

It was stupid, she thought, to be nervous. After all, she wanted to swim, and it was a perfect night with a warm breeze. Probably the exercise would be just what she needed in order to get a good night's sleep. How ridiculous her hesitation was. It wasn't as if they were in some remote place. There were a few people strolling above them on the path that overlooked the ocean.

Finally Penny slipped out of her slacks, folding them neatly and placing them next to Joel's clothes. She sat down on the rocky beach to remove her sandals, thinking how considerate he had been to undress first and leave her. Stretching her long, shapely legs out in front of her, she threw her head back, staring up into the starry sky. Her body glowed in the silver light, and she could not have guessed that the picture that registered in Joel Sanborne's mind as he gazed at her was that of a metallic nymphette, a languid, mythical creature lost on the shore, praying to her lost people.

Suddenly Penny leaped to her feet and ran toward the sea, trying not to think of what an unlikely experience this was. The hot air caressed her scantily clad body. Was it possible that the moonlight had burned her?

"Dive through the waves!" Joel shouted. "Once you get out here the swimming's great."

Penny followed his directions, gulping for air, sputtering as the salty water coursed over her face. Although she was a strong swimmer she was relieved that there was scarcely any undertow. With an amazed grin she surfaced, her hair slicked back, her body poised like a young animal's. Never in her life had she felt such exhilaration, such power in the force of her own body. She wondered if the wine she had had for dinner was causing a delayed reaction, for she did not feel like her old cautious self, but felt rather as if she had just burst from the womb, just been born into a vivid new existence.

Joel waded toward her, the water just above his waist. "God, you look beautiful. Do you have any idea?" He stared at her.

"Like a drowned rat," Penny gasped self-consciously and dived under the water. A strong hand caught her arm, pulling her back to the surface.

"You should always wear your hair wet . . . or at least pulled back away from your face." He tilted her chin up, smiling down

42

at her. "And I have nothing against glasses, but what a shame to hide those wide, green, cat eyes."

Oh, he was close, far too close, and she felt smothered. Here in the open sea air it seemed she could not breathe. She laughed, a bubbly, breathless, new laugh which sounded foreign to her. "It's the latest style, you know. The *wet* look. Really, I saw it in a French *Vogue*. Women are greasing their hair . . . can you imagine? I wouldn't want to put grease on my . . ."

She broke off the wild chatter abruptly. She *never* chattered like that. It was as if she was possessed, as if another, more dynamic spirit had taken control of her. She dived off again, swimming hard, her heart pounding. She felt as though she could swim the ocean. The energy that coursed through her had to find an outlet, so she swam on and on without looking back, just swimming straight ahead with occasional glances over her left shoulder to make certain she was going along parallel with the shore.

"Stop!" She heard his command disintegrate into deep laughter. "Penny, stop swimming or we'll be halfway to Boston."

She stopped then, blinking and gasping and holding her right side where there was a dull stab from the overexertion. Panting, she swam toward the shore until the water was only up to her knees. Then she collapsed, throwing herself back into the water, allowing her body to go completely limp. She closed her eyes and heard the water part as he swam up next to her. In the silence there was only the sound of her labored breathing, the sound of the surf. She felt his hands around her waist as he lifted her, turning her body over until she was lying flat on her back, floating effortlessly as he balanced her with his two hands gently touching the small of her back. He moved her body back and forth, back and forth, until she felt herself almost hypnotized by the undulating movement. Softly he began to hum, a lullabylike melody, still gliding her body through the water, making the sound of ripples against her skin.

Dimly she felt him lift her again. His hands held her securely under her arms, and as he raised her body out of the salty surf she felt his thumbs against her breasts. He held her up like a child against the starry sky, her long legs dangling, only her toes submerged. They were both bathed in moonlight, dripping and breathless as two primeval creatures from the sea. The look in his eye told her that he was as stunned by the poetic timelessness of this moment as she was.

Then, ever so slowly, he began to lower her nymphlike body. She placed her hands on his slippery shoulders, clutching at him in an agonized ecstasy as each part of her body skimmed against his . . . her breasts slid past his forehead, felt the sharpness of his nose; his lips nipped lightly as he lowered her. And all the while his dark eyes held hers, signaling to her a desire so shattering in its intensity that her mind was blank.

Penny inhaled a slow breath, and her body quivered as the waters lapped around her waist. As Joel's mouth sought hers she felt the entire force of his being melting into her. She steadied her feet on the rocky ocean bottom and slid her hands from his shoulders to his chest. Her fingers studied the wiry hairs that were confined to one small patch in the center of his torso. Her hands between them now were intent on those two hard pellets that were his nipples. He moaned as she took one between her thumb and forefinger.

Suddenly she felt his passion unleashed, and his kiss, so gentle at first, was demanding something more as his tongue, like lightning, burned into her mouth in sharp, searching jabs. She heard a moan, piercing against the splashing surf, and it was seconds before she recognized the sound of her own voice calling his name.

Where was she? In the night with Joel Sanborne, embraced by the sea as his hands like water wings flew down the sides of her quivering body. She knew it was madness, but at the same time she was aware of a deep security within herself. She felt safe here, complete. As his tongue surged deeper into her mouth she tasted the salt of the sea combined with the wine they had shared at dinner. It was a delicious combination, and she drank in more and more of what he offered so willingly.

She relished the hardness of his chest as it pushed against her breasts, flattening them, molding them into his throbbing body. His heart beat wildy, and the fury raging through his body ignited her. Soon there would be no turning back.

Now beneath the water his muscular thighs pressed against hers. She squeezed her eyes shut at the glorious shudder that ran through his body when she eased her legs apart. She arched back and opened her eyes to see the stars spinning above her. Joel's mouth sucked hungrily into her neck, and with so many delicious sensations assaulting her she felt herself close to screaming. Her arms were around his neck, clinging, her nails digging into his wet, slippery skin. Once again he lifted her up, but this time he pulled her legs around him so that they encircled his waist. All the while his tongue was chasing hers, seeking out new hollows, finding new rhythms.

She could not tear her mouth away from his, and when he carried her into shallower water she wondered vaguely why she could make no move to stop him. She heard his husky voice whispering some outrageous flattery, but it was all like a dream, a dream that the warm August breeze had blown in from another rare, exotic continent. Sensation after sensation collided inside her body, spinning a web of fire that spread into her mind as well. Her entire spirit seemed to be aroused by this man, this all-knowing, powerful mystery whose touch transported her into exaltation. She rode him like a willing rider until they were nearly to the shore. Once, only once, she tried to stop that interminable kiss, but not wanting to . . . she could not.

Her body grew more supple, pliant, and eager as his hands burned over her. She unwound her long legs from around his waist, and he eased her to her feet. The water was only up to their ankles here, and the bottom was sandy. Again he eased his cool thigh between her legs.

"Stop . . . Joel . . . someone might see us . . ." She pressed her legs tightly together to stop him.

"There's no one here." His voice was husky. She felt his warm,

45

harsh breaths against her cool skin as he supported her with one hand placed against the small of her back.

"I know but . . ." Penny squirmed, but he silenced her with a searing kiss that made the ocean come alive inside her. Her whole body was undulating against him with the rhythm of the sea. The air was cool on her wet skin, and now that they were standing out of the water his hands which swept lightly down her body were like the wind or like feathers.

She told herself it was all right. They were two people kissing on a public beach . . . just kissing here in the shadows with perhaps a few people strolling by on the promenade above them.

But now she sensed that those cunning hands of his had banished all reason. Something else had overtaken her, and her body felt a need to crash, to fulfill the restlessness his hands had created. She moaned as his hand slipped inside her bikini top massaging one of her breasts until the nipple grew hard, until she thought she would explode. Now Joel was shuddering uncontrollably; they were leaning into each other in a daze of desire. He tugged at the top of her bikini until one breast spilled out into his hand, and then his mouth covered it, licking and coaxing until the whole front of her body felt on fire.

Penny buried her head against his chest, struggling unwillingly with the knowledge that soon they would have to stop. Involuntarily it seemed her lips began to caress his shoulder. At that moment his hand deserted her breast and skillfully slid down the side of her body. She felt his palm rest momentarily against her thigh, then as if he had gathered courage, his fingers inched stealthily under the bottom of her bikini.

Again she wondered what she was doing. How was this happening? She forced herself to grab his hand, forcing it out from under the thin, cotton bikini. Against her will she heard her voice say no, no, and no again. But he was scooping her up into his arms, carrying her back onto the beach into a secluded area, away from the eyes of midnight strollers.

He lowered her to the blanket and towel he had spread out earlier, and his hand, warm and dry now, stroked her abdomen.

46

"Joel . . . please . . ." To her utter astonishment her voice held no finality. Her weakness infuriated her, and she struggled to find someplace within herself where she might finally resist him. She wanted him. There was no question about that, and with his body, the full weight of him resting on top of her now, she knew beyond question how desperately he wanted her.

"Oh . . . Penny . . . Penny." His moan was a tortured cry; his hand pulled back her hair yet she felt no pain.

His weight was like a gift; she received it gladly, marveling in the perfection she felt as she held him. He framed her face with his hands, and the look of awe she had seen once before came into his eyes. He smoothed her hair until she felt it slicked back against her head like a cap. She did not want to move, wanted this warm, liquid feeling to go on forever.

He brought his face to within inches of hers, and she closed her eyes, savoring the last moments of this new bliss.

Again his hand, so knowingly, so naturally, caressed her stomach. She stirred beneath him, yeilding to the pressure as he slipped his hand beneath the green and white fabric and began vanquishing her with soft strokes, smoothing her until her legs parted involuntarily and she cried out.

"My beautiful girl. My beautiful Penny."

She arched against his foraging hand. No, it wasn't real. Joel Sanborne could not be saying those words to her, and if he was saying them he could not be meaning them. She grasped his dark hair in one hand and threw her body forward. There were no rocks beneath her, there was nothing beneath her now.

## CHAPTER THREE

The drive back to Marblehead was tense and silent. Joel pounded out an angry, emphatic rhythm on the dashboard with one hand while the other hand expertly guided the cream-colored Porsche around the coastal curves. Penny, feeling as trite as a callow, inexperienced teen-ager, clung to the opposite side of the car, trying to think of a way to breach the gap that had come between them when she had finally pulled away from him on the beach.

Penny's protests echoed in her ears as she glanced surreptitiously at Joel's stony profile. Inside her head the words came easily. She had not protested out of prudery; surely he could have seen that. Surely he knew how much she had responded to those fiery kisses, to the tender coaxing of his strangely gentle hands. Surely he knew all that but . . . didn't he see it was too soon? Yes, of course they had known each other for several years. That is, they had known each other well enough to say hello, but that was hardly knowing. The Joel Sanborne she was coming to know was, or seemed to be, totally different from the suave television personality she had come to think of as Buck Handlin.

But although Penny's mind was full of all of the logical, heartfelt reasons she wanted to give him, she remained silent. Her stomach churned as they entered the sleepy village of Marblehead. She could not let it end this way! Only what if she spoke out and he laughed? What if he was sitting there now not even worrying about her rejection? Probably it was unusual for him to "fail" with a woman, but it must have happened sometime in his long, amorous career. No doubt he had the confidence to withstand such a petty, insignificant rejection as Penny had just dealt him!

Penny closed her eyes against so many negative thoughts. She was beginning again to think of him as the callous Buck Handlin and not as the sensitive, enthusiastic man who had taken her to dinner that first night in Marblehead.

As Joel pulled up in front of the New England Yacht Club she forced herself to speak.

"I feel terrible." Her voice reflected absolutely the truth of her statement.

"Join the crowd." Joel switched off the ignition but made no move to get out of the Porsche.

"I . . . I had a wonderful time this evening . . . I mean before. I mean . . . I even had a. . . . It's hard for me to explain."

"Try," Joel said tightly.

Penny stared straight ahead, wishing herself out of the situation and at the same time, on some deeper level, yearning for a solution that would bring back the closeness they had felt earlier.

"Okay," she said finally. "I may as well just say what I'm thinking. It couldn't make matters worse."

Joel turned to her, and his eyes were dark and brooding. Once again she fought back the sensation that she was dealing with Buck Handlin.

"I like you," she blurted out. "I do . . . and I'm surprised I do. I never knew you before we came to Marblehead. Back in New York I made it a point to stay out of your way. I . . . I guess I was afraid of you."

"Afraid?" A look of dismay flickered in Joel's brooding gaze.

"I was afraid," Penny said, rushing on and trying not to censor her words. "You see, I have this silly idea that I'm unique. I know I don't act it or dress it, but I've always thought of myself

49

as a person who is a good judge of people. Buck Handlin is . . . is a horrible man. He's not my type . . . always slapping his women around—"

"But . . ." Joel started to interrupt, but Penny grasped his hand urgently as she went on.

"I know you're not Buck. I mean, I know it *now*. Before that I was confused, and mostly I guess I was confused about *my* reaction to you. You see, I knew I hated Buck . . . even though I think your portrayal of him is sensitive and remarkable. He is to be pitied . . . he's neurotic and self-destructive. I pity him, but I sure wouldn't want to become involved with him."

"Wait a minute!" Joel exclaimed. "I'm not him! What are you saying?"

"I'm saying"—Penny tightened her hands into fists—"the reason I avoided you at the studio was because I was attracted to you. I didn't like myself for it because I guess I felt I was attracted to Buck. And . . . and I'm afraid of being like all the other women in your life."

"But you"—Joel moved his face close to hers and his eyes burned angrily—"you don't know anything about *my* life."

"I know." Penny met his eyes steadily.

"You really think I'm like that monster, Buck?" Joel questioned hoarsely.

Penny shook her head vehemently. "Not anymore . . . but I was confused. Please understand."

Joel frowned as he climbed out of the Porsche. He kicked at the gravel, then glanced out at the sea with a weary expression. "I'm sick of Buck Handlin."

Penny walked silently at his side, sensing a deep depression in him that went beyond what had transpired between them earlier. Oddly, she felt that unwittingly she had hurt him deeply. How strange that this man she had believed to be so impervious to the opinions of others proved to be as vulnerable as, say, someone like Irene, who was just beginning her career as an actress. Somehow seeing this vulnerability moved Penny deeply. She wanted to make it right for him. Seeing him so miserable was just unbearable.

"Joel . . . we're just getting to know each other. Probably I've blundered and said everything wrong but . . . I wouldn't want it to . . . to halt our . . . friendship."

"Don't worry." Joel shook his head darkly, but his words did not dispel her fear.

"This is an important opportunity for me," Penny said softly as they approached their rooms. "You were kidding me about being the type who didn't mix business with pleasure but . . . that's right. Only . . . I didn't count on having such fun with you. I . . . I just can't afford to complicate my life during these next two weeks. I want to be in top form in case Max needs me to direct some scenes."

Joel nodded tightly. "I understand."

But he didn't. Penny could practically see the protective shell forming around him.

"I thought we could just . . . go slow," she said in a final attempt.

"Don't worry." Joel leaned over and gave her a cool peck on the cheek, then he let himself inside his own room and she heard him lock the door.

The next day they were shooting just outside Marblehead in a rambling Victorian mansion replete with widow's walks and gingerbread latticework. They would be filming at the mansion for the rest of the week, and since the day was overcast with a good chance of a storm, Max had phoned Penny at six in the morning to inform her that they would take advantage of the possibly foul weather and alter the schedule to begin shooting interiors.

Penny had immediately phoned the actors to tell them they would not be needed on location until ten o'clock, which would give them time to learn their lines for the scenes to be shot that day. By eight Penny was bumping along in the van with the other members of the technical crew and their equipment. In a way it

51

was good that this sudden change had come up because there was no time to think of Joel and last night's ill-fated swim. When she had phoned him earlier with the change in schedule, he had been pleasant but nothing more. So perhaps from here on in it would be strictly business. As the van ground to a halt in front of the old sea mansion, Penny sloshed the rest of her coffee on her jeans and swore under her breath as she hopped out.

Max had put her in charge of setting up shots for the first scene, which was to take place in the luxurious Oriental-carpeted bedroom of the old mansion. Penny and the cameramen joked about the ghoulish nature of the mansion—the place did have an eerie, stale quality. Apparently it had been on the real estate market for four years without a single offer. But it was appropriate for the scene in which Joel, as Buck Handlin was to sneak into the bedroom of his former wife, played by Tippy Malone, and force himself on her.

By ten the actors were sitting on the carpeted staircase outside the bedroom, sipping morning coffee and reading their newspapers. Penny tried not to look at Joel as he shared his Boston *Globe* with Tippy, who was already costumed in an alluring, diaphanous peignoir.

"Darling, come look at this!" Just as Penny was about to take a coffee break herself, Faye Barker called her over to give her opinion of Tippy's makeup. Penny's stomach tightened as she approached the show's delicately beautiful leading lady, who was still seated on the staircase with one hand casually resting on Joel's knee. Penny tried to think of something brisk and clever to say and was relieved when Joel tossed a cheerful good morning meant for both her and Faye.

"Faye says I need more eyeshadow." Tippy blinked her long dark lashes at Penny. "I'm supposed to be in bed. Asleep. I'm supposed to be bushed from a day of sailing and sound asleep when Buck breaks into my bedroom. I am not supposed to be dripping with mascara. Don't you agree, Penny?"

"Well"—Penny grasped Faye Barker's chubby arm—"she's right, Faye. This is not the ball scene."

"No, no, no." Faye tossed her bronze curls and shook a finger in Tippy's face. Faye adored Tippy, but they were forever haggling over mascara. "She shouldn't look like a corpse, is all I'm saying. But she won't let me put even a smidge on her. And we can't run this tape back and do it over if it ain't right."

"Everybody knows that, Faye," Tippy said and smiled sweetly.

"Don't get smart," snapped Faye, and Penny bit back a smile. The scene was all a part of a familiar ritual. Everyone involved with *Dream of Life* knew that Faye could not get through a day without a problem of some sort, but they loved her in spite of it. The challenge, thought Penny, was to let Faye think her problem was of vast importance and then to convince her that she herself had solved the problem that she herself had created.

"Let's see how she looks under the lights in the bedroom." Penny caught Tippy's eye in a meaningful look, and the three women marched into the high-ceilinged boudoir with its mammoth canopied four-poster bed and its French doors that overlooked the tumultuous gray ocean.

"Reminds me of Wuthering Heights," Tippy commented as she slid beneath the covers and propped herself up on the satin pillows.

Faye and Penny stood across the room evaluating Tippy's makeup.

"You're right," Penny whispered. "She's too pale."

"Ya see." Faye knit her red eyebrows into a satisfied scowl. "She's a stubborn little thing. Always giving me trouble and all I want is for her to look good. You'd think I was against her, the way she acts."

"I know," Penny soothed. "But with the last-minute change in the shooting schedule she's under a lot of pressure."

"My God, she looks pale as a ghost." Faye smacked her lips. "I could put a darker base on her too."

"We got to get on with it!" Max burst into the bedroom. "If there's an electrical storm, we could lose power."

"Great!" shouted one of the cameramen. "Then we'll really be ahead of schedule."

"Serge, I don't need any jokes." Max smiled despite the tension he felt himself to be under. "Penny, is everything set up? I want to do the love scene between Tippy and Joel first, then we can cut back and pick up the shots of Joel breaking into the room. Tippy won't have to hang around that way. You feeling okay, sweetheart?"

Tippy nodded at Max as she slithered down beneath the covers.

"I told you she didn't look good," Faye whispered to Penny.

"Faye," Penny drew the older woman aside. "You're absolutely right about Tippy's makeup, but we just can't take the time for you to do a whole job. What can you do to fix it . . . quick?"

Faye screwed her face into a wrinkled mass of thinking nerves and decided that loosening Tippy's dark hair from its tidy chignon would soften her appearance. After that a touch of mascara to the outer lashes would create the perfect effect.

"Great!" Penny reported the decision to an amicable Tippy and, script in hand, moved to Max's side for further instructions.

Archie Marshall, who was acting as stage manager, held up the slate with the scene number chalked on it, and Max called for quiet on the set. Penny caught her breath as Joel moved to his position leaning over the sleeping Tippy. He leaned forward, brushing his cheek lightly over Tippy's dark hair. Then, as her eyes flew open in panic, he slipped his hand beneath the covers.

"Buck!" Tippy cried out, and as she tried to leap out of bed, Joel caught her scantily clad body and drew her roughly against him.

"You know damn well you never stopped wanting me!" And before Tippy could utter her next line he fell on top of her diminutive form, caressing her pale shoulder as their lips met in a long kiss.

Serge was moving in for a close-up, and there was absolute stillness in the room. Joel moaned and spoke his next line as a hungry demand. Penny's pulse was racing, her breath was coming in short gasps, and she realized with a sense of shock that her body was responding to everything that Joel was doing to Tippy. She glanced furtively around the room, but all other eyes were glued to the writhing couple on the bed. A dizziness came over Penny, and she backed up to a chaise and sank gratefully down. She could not tear her eyes away from Joel and Tippy.

"You never wanted me out of your life." Joel's large hands practically covered Tippy's trembling body.

"No . . . I didn't." Tippy ran one finger along his face until it came to rest on his chin.

As Joel lowered his face for another kiss, it seemed to Penny she could taste the salt of last night's kisses on the beach. She could almost feel his hands sweeping along her body, covering her breasts, making her feel more alive than she had ever felt.

But it was so easy for him to make love. Penny tore her eyes away as Joel removed his shirt and ran his hands through Tippy's thick black hair. Tippy laughed and suddenly the scene, as dictated by the script, turned light and playful. Penny felt a surge of jealousy so extreme that it was all she could do to remain in the room. She stood up, her arms rigid at her sides.

"You haven't changed," Joel said with a laugh as he leaned over Tippy, playfully nipping at her cheek.

"How did you know where to find me?" By now Tippy was a disheveled but even more alluring sight. Penny felt her own body turn to lead as she watched Tippy's graceful gestures and listened to her beguiling laughter. So what if Tippy lied about her age. She was beautiful with her creamy, flawless complexion and naturally dark lashes. Of course, Tippy had been right. She had not needed more mascara. Damn her!

Penny turned away, appalled at the irrational jealousy she was experiencing. Her whole life seemed to have been turned around, jumbled beyond comprehension. She moved silently to a far corner of the room where she could scarcely hear any of the dialogue that was being spoken between Tippy and Joel. She had better get hold of herself, or the rest of the remote was going to be a miserable experience.

"Cut!" Max's scream interrupted her thoughts. "I want to run that through once more, you two." Max hopped across the heavy camera cables and sat down on the bed to speak to his two stars.

Again? Penny felt an uncommon meanness of spirit at the idea of having to watch the love scene for a second time. Damn Max! He should have had everything he wanted from the last take, and here he was playing director, chatting it up with Tippy and Joel. Directors love love scenes. Penny walked out into the hall fuming and poured herself a cup of the wretchedly acidic coffee from the canteen. She picked up a stale cherry danish and bit into it with a vengeance. She felt uncharitable and mean and she hated herself for it.

"How goes it?" Archie sat down beside her on the staircase.

"Fine," Penny said and nodded curtly.

"Not convincing." Archie's blue eyes were full of sympathy, but Penny was not deceived.

Actors, she thought. Who could trust them? They *were* actors after all, and they were capable of turning their emotions on and off. Today's events had certainly taught her a lot—she certainly realized now that the last thing in the world she wanted was to be married to an actor. Married? Penny shook her head irritably. Now where did that idea come from?

She looked back at Archie with the same irritable expression. "I get this way before storms," she said tightly and was more irritated when he laughed at what he thought was a joke.

She moved away from Archie to a window that overlooked the ocean. She wished it would storm, wished the thunder would interrupt or the lightning would strike a power line. If she could have the rest of the day to herself to think things through, then she would be able to get control of herself.

"Penny!" Max was standing in the door that led to the bedroom. He motioned urgently for her to come, then pressed a piece of paper into her hand.

"A prescription for Tippy. She's not feeling well. If she doesn't perk up, we're done for the day."

Penny grabbed an umbrella and left the mansion grumbling uncharitably about Tippy and hystrionics and hypochondria and star complexes and life in general.

"Hey, I'll drive in with you!" She winced as Archie jumped into the passenger seat of the van.

She was inside the pharmacy waiting for Tippy's prescription to be filled when the first crack of thunder sounded. Good, she thought, an afternoon off to cool down.

The elderly pharmacist was taking his time. Penny wandered over to the magazine rack and leafed mindlessly through a day-time TV fan magazine. Under the best of circumstances it was difficult to maintain a long-term relationship. Imagine how difficult it would be to be married to an actor, especially a sexy, handsome actor like Joel Sanborne. My God, there would always be women clamoring after him. And there would always be love scenes to be played with other women.

Penny shivered as if a blast of icy air had swept through the drugstore. Watching Joel make love to Tippy had drained her. How did she know they were only acting? Could she ever be sure? Could she ever be confident enough to marry a man whom millions of other women considered their personal property? No wonder there were so many divorces in the entertainment world.

Penny replaced the fan magazine with a frown. She didn't know the exact statistics. It would be interesting to know for sure if actors had a higher divorce rate or if it was simply that their marriages received greater publicity.

Suddenly questions that had never before entered her mind were overwhelming her. Why on earth was she thinking about long-term relationships with actors when, after last night, there wasn't the remotest possibility that Joel would be interested in her?

And why did she care? She scowled as she took the receipt from the pharmacist.

A second crack of thunder brought down a deluge, but as she

darted out of the pharmacy Archie thrust the umbrella over her head and, grabbing her arm, guided her to the van.

"Thanks." She forced a smile as he opened the door for her. It had not escaped her attention that he had held her more intimately than she would have liked.

She declined his offer to drive and after wiping her glasses off on his handkerchief drove back to the mansion with a new sense of determination to stick strictly to business.

"I hope this helps Tippy." She removed the keys from the ignition and smiled at Archie. She really had been rather curt with him. Perhaps in her present mood she had imagined everything.

As she started to get out of the van Archie reached across the front seat and took her arm. "You're a beautiful woman." He leaned toward her, and she was so taken aback by this blatant gesture that she could only stare at him.

"I think we could have a real good time, you and me." He entwined his fingers in hers and raised her hand to his lips and kissed it.

"What are you doing?" Penny snapped.

Archie froze at her candid rebuke and then smiled smoothly as if nothing had happened. "Paying you a compliment. Shall we make a run for it?"

Penny tossed him the umbrella and hopped out of the van. "You take the umbrella. It would be a shame if you caught cold."

She was drenched to the bone by the time she got back inside. Serge and Faye were in the foyer smoking cigarettes and speaking in low whispers.

"At least we didn't lose power." Penny threw them a smile as she mounted the stairs.

"Tippy fainted," Serge called after her. "Max drove her back to the Yacht Club, so that's it for today."

"No!" Penny wheeled around, exasperated. Faye and Serge nodded simultaneously. "Couldn't we have done another scene?

58

He could have picked up the shots of Joel in the hallway and then entering the room. My God, we could have done something!"

Suddenly the idea of having the rest of the day off loomed in front of her. She sank to the stairs, elbows on her knees, her chin in her hands.

"Max is worried about Tippy." Faye smashed out her cigarette and came to sit down by Penny.

"She seemed fine when she was doing the bed scene with Joel." Penny winced at the sharp tone in her voice, but neither Faye nor Serge gave any indication of noticing.

"The call is for six tomorrow morning," Serge said, "no matter what the weather does. Max thinks we can finish the interiors by noon and then move out front for the car sequence. The light should be fine in the late afternoon."

Penny shook her head dismally, and Faye patted her on the back. "So go back to your room and put on dry clothes and come with us to the Witch House."

"The what?" Penny queried.

"The Witch House in Salem," Serge explained. "Faye is organizing a tour."

"Bein' as I'm a witch." Faye shimmied her shoulders and tried to smile wickedly at Penny.

Penny grinned. "Okay. I need to be distracted. I guess witches are as good a way as any."


By the time they returned from Salem and Faye's witch tour, the storm had passed and the late-afternoon sun was sparkling on the waters. Penny asked to be let out in the center of Marblehead, and as she was crossing the street to pick up some yogurt in the little market, she spotted Archie and Irene strolling arm in arm along the footpath that wound down to the water's edge. So Archie was now making a play for naïve little Irene. Penny doubted very much if Irene even knew that Archie was the "happily married" type.

Without the noisy camaraderie of Faye and the others, Penny's mind once again started veering off to thoughts of Joel. In order to stave off those unwelcome thoughts she wandered into a dusty old bookstore and spent the next hour and a half browsing through obscure old volumes. She ended up buying a worn leather volume of Edgar Allan Poe stories and, feeling a sense of macabre satisfaction, left the bookstore with the intention of spending a scary night reading in bed. But she was relieved in a sense to spot Irene sitting alone in the little outdoor café in the center of the village.

"Join me," shouted Irene.

"What a day." Penny collapsed in the chair beside her and ordered a glass of wine.

"Yeah." Irene said, nodding. "Archie told me Tippy fainted."

Penny shook her head and after pondering a moment decided she owed Irene some of the recently gleaned information about Archie "Good Guy" Marshall.

"No!" Irene shrieked when Penny told her about the pass Archie had made at her in the van. "He just invited me to drive in to Boston to go to this fabulous restaurant." Irene raised an eyebrow impishly. "Do you think he caught me on the rebound from you?"

Penny chuckled. "I think he is definitely in the market for a partner, and really, Irene, what you do is your business, but I thought you ought to know. Did you know he was married?"

Irene drew her mouth into a quick pout. "He told me he was separated."

Penny shrugged. "I was at his apartment for dinner two weeks ago. He didn't seem separated then."

"He's too old for me anyway," Irene said with a giggle.

"You're not disappointed that I told you?" asked Penny.

"I'm glad!" exclaimed Irene. "I don't like messy things. I mean I'd like to have a boyfriend and all that, but not someone who's already married."

"And who has two terrific daughters," Penny added.

"Isn't it weird." Irene shook her head ingenuously, "I mean, he must have known I'd find out. Or maybe he thought I knew and didn't care. I guess he probably thought that. Sometimes guys think I'm dumb because I smile a lot."

"You're just happy." Penny smiled. She was glad she'd run into Irene. The more she knew of the little blonde, the more she liked her. There was an appealing, uncluttered honesty about Irene that was refreshing.

"You know who's really nice?" Irene leaned forward with a conspirator's smile. "Joel Sanborne."

"Yes." Penny caught her breath and smiled.

"He has a good sense of humor," Irene observed with a crooked smile at Penny.

"Oh, he does. Yes, he's nice."

"You think I should"—Irene paused dramatically—"try to get his attention?"

"If that's what you want, Irene, then definitely you should. He . . . he seems like a very generous, honest, and sensitive man. I mean he is glamorous and all, but somehow he's not phony."

Irene burst suddenly into laughter, and Penny regarded her quizzically.

"I think you're in love with him," Irene whispered devilishly.

"I am not!" Penny protested too loudly and Irene laughed harder. "What makes you say that?" she questioned with a sinking sensation.

"I saw you two together the first night we arrived . . . and then I saw the way you looked at him and the way he looked at you and—"

"What do you mean the way he looked at me?" Penny interrupted urgently.

"He looks at you all the time," Irene said smugly.

"He does not!" Penny felt a quiver of excitement in the pit of her stomach.

"You're too busy to notice," Irene went on. "He's always looking at you."

*He's always looking at you.* Irene's words echoed in Penny's mind all during dinner that evening. Irene's observation had been sincere enough, but maybe her overactive imagination had overpowered her. *He's always looking at you.* Again and again Penny replayed those words, and after she said good night to Irene and was on her way back to her own room to settle in with Mr. Poe, she sat down on an old park bench and thought about the implication of those words. Could it be possible that Joel had noticed her, had felt something for her prior to coming to Marblehead? Was it possible that they had both felt the same attraction even before that first night together?

Penny's pulse quickened. Why did that possibility infuse her with such optimism? She reminded herself of all the conflicting emotions she had felt upon seeing Tippy in his arms, but the excitement and sense of optimism continued.

At that moment she spotted Joel, his hands shoved into the pockets of his beige trousers, walking slowly across the lawn toward his room. Impulsively she called his name and hurried across the lawn toward him. He smiled, but his eyes were wary.

Penny swallowed hard and then heard herself saying. "It's an early call tomorrow which means we'll be through by three and I saw an interesting art gallery in Marblehead and thought you might want to take a look with me."

Joel's face softened, and he stared at her incredulously with such warmth that she felt her cheeks flush.

"Fine," he replied, nodding slowly, his eyes still warm on her face.

"If you finish before me . . . I'll meet you there."

"I know the gallery," he said, a touch of awe still in his voice.

"Well . . . good night." Penny turned the key in her lock, and her heart was pounding.

He took her hand and turned her back around until she was facing him. "Thanks." His face broke into a broad smile.

Penny nodded and her own face broke into a relaxed grin. "I never did that before," she admitted.

"I'm glad you did." Joel drew her to him, and his soft full lips pressed against hers until every part of her body yearned to be touched by him. She wrapped her arms around his neck and allowed her fingers to wander through his thick coarse hair. She

62

marveled at the texture of his hair as if she had never felt anything like it. She closed her eyes to intensify the sensation and as she did, her senses were bombarded by his fragrence, which was fresh sea and salt with a hint of the citron cologne she had detected earlier in the evening. How desperately she longed to explore every detail of this fascinating man. With a sense of caution she moved her hands from his tangled hair down the smooth muscles of his neck and onto his broad shoulders.

Now that the sensation of his lean chest pressing into her breasts was a familiar one, it was all the more wondrous, all the more exciting and dear to her. It was Joel, Joel's tenderness and uniqueness that she felt throbbing into her. When his tongue made quick darting forays into her mouth, she answered him with the new and deeper knowledge she had of him.

And it seemed to be the same for him. They wanted so much from each other and the wanting was endless, endless and ever increasing. This, she thought, was a man to grow with, a man to learn from, a man to surprise. A man who would accept her surprises. Penny responded hungrily to his moist, searching kisses. There was an inevitability to their lovemaking now, and they both seemed to be savoring the delicious postponement of that final act.

They pulled apart bleary-eyed and stood gasping, their eyes riveted, unable to utter a single word. Joel traced his forefinger along the line of her eyebrow, down the side of her face, and onto her lips. She parted her lips and sucked delicately on his finger. The mad urgency they had felt earlier had been replaced by a warm, delicious feeling of suspense.

He bent to kiss her, and she felt the chasteness of that kiss as an even deeper, more profound form of seduction. His patience stirred her, and she ran her hands lightly down his chest.

"Don't take too many chances," he said with a mock flinch.

"Sorry." She removed her hands and smiled at him. The knowledge he had of her was comforting as well as exciting. She basked in the warmth of his half smile.

"Tomorrow." He brushed his lips against her cheek, then

unable to leave it at that, she felt his warm breath on her neck, his long, sensuous tongue curling around her ear. She shivered with delight and gave his hand a squeeze.

"How am I going to sleep?" he whispered.

"How am *I* going to sleep?" she echoed.

He hugged her, and they stood for a moment with their arms around each other. How wonderful it was not to play games. How incredibly easy it was for her to let him know that her desire for him matched his own. She smiled against his bulk . . . as if he hadn't been able to guess by her responses.

"Sweet dreams." He gave her bottom a light pat, and when she turned back to him from inside her room, he waved good night to her with a smile that was a promise.

# CHAPTER FOUR

"Tomorrow" arrived bathed in sunny splendor, and the work on the set reflected its perfection. Penny arrived promptly at six, and minutes later a much less harried Max arrived to say he had given Tippy permission to catch a couple of extra hours of sleep, so they would begin filming Joel's stealthy entrance into the mansion and his appearance in Tippy's bedchamber.

Although she was not technically directing Joel's work, Max seemed eager for Penny's suggestions, and for the first time since the remote had begun she had a real sense of creative accomplishment. Joel was in high spirits and joked with the crew between takes. By the time Tippy arrived they had completed not only the scheduled takes but had actually skipped ahead and filmed a scene between Archie, Irene, and Joel that was not on the schedule for another three days. Max was exuberant, and Tippy, sensing everyone's "high," rose to the occasion. Her work with Joel far surpassed that of the previous day.

Although Joel made no mention of their date later that afternoon, Penny caught him staring at her several times. Between takes in the love scene with Tippy he was somehow always at her side, chatting casually with her and Faye, joking about the soggy danish, or pointing out an interesting piece in the Boston *Globe*.

Much to her surprise Penny was able to watch Tippy and Joel writhing away on the four-poster from a completely objective point of view. Later that afternoon, after she and Joel had visited the art gallery and were sitting on the outside patio of one of the restaurants that overlooked the sea, she confessed the frightful emotions she had experienced the day before.

"It was horrible," Penny concluded. "I'd always liked Tippy . . . until yesterday; but it was too bizarre to stand there and watch the two of you."

Joel nodded with a sardonic smile. "My ex-wife would agree with you. She never got used to it."

Penny sipped her white wine and stared out at the smooth sea. She was well aware that by mentioning her reaction to the love scene she was revealing something of herself, something of her feelings for Joel. Yet the realization did not make her nervous. Joel seemed almost glad that she had brought up the subject.

"It's a liability," he said finally. "Maybe it's impossible for people in my profession to have an enduring relationship."

"Do you really believe that?" asked Penny.

Joel considered her question with a far-off melancholy look. "Let's say I'm not eager to find out."

Penny's spirits flagged, yet there was something in his tone that made her think that while he might not be eager to fall in love or form some permanent bond with a woman, he deeply wanted to believe such a relationship was possible.

"But I didn't feel those same . . . jealous, primitive feelings today," Penny persisted. "And . . . and I think it's because yesterday I was all jangled from the argument we'd had the night before. I don't know . . ." She broke off, blushing. Wasn't she revealing too much?

"What?" Joel reached across the table and took her hand. He squeezed it gently, urging her to continue.

Penny glanced into his dark eyes and was moved by the intensity of his anticipation. He wanted to know. He *needed* to know what she thought!

"Today," she continued tentatively, "you kept coming over

and talking to me. It's silly, I guess, but . . . I felt in some way connected to you, so that seeing that same scene today was a totally different experience."

Joel's dark eyes searched her face with an intensity that made her feel he was looking into her very soul. "You're an extraordinary person," he said finally, and Penny laughed to cover her embarrassment.

"No, you really are," he insisted as his finger began tracing the tiny veins in her hand. "You don't play games. You say what you think. It makes things a lot easier."

Penny felt a flutter of delight at the compliment and wondered if she should tell him that she had never in her life been able to be so honest and open with a man as she had been with him, that much to her surprise and almost in spite of herself he seemed able to draw out the real Penny, the Penny she wanted to be.

"Actually I wasn't a very good husband," he admitted suddenly. "We were only married for two years, and I gave her several good reasons to be as miserable as she was."

Penny nodded and waited for him to continue. Somehow his confession did not frighten her—perhaps because for the past three years she had seen the numerous women come and go in his life, and was not in the least surprised that his philandering had contributed to the failure of his marriage.

"But you've never been married?" he questioned.

Penny shook her head and he smiled slyly as he released her hand. "Too busy working?"

"Partly," she confessed. "I always thought I'd like to at least have my directing career underway before taking on any other obligations."

"Obligations?" He seemed skeptical.

"Yes, I think love or . . . or marriage is an obligation. It takes work just like a career."

"How did you grow so wise?" Joel grinned and picked up her hand again. "You're too pretty to be an owl, but you do possess several owlish attributes."

Penny laughed and pushed her glasses down on her nose to peer at him.

"What time is your call tomorrow morning?" Joel leaned across the table with one of Buck Handlin's most seductive smiles.

A violent wave of desire swept over her, something that had never before happened to her, something that felt utterly out of her control. His eyes held hers, and beneath the small table she felt his muscular leg insert itself firmly between her legs, which were clad in tight, faded jeans. He cupped her hand in his, and as his leg pressed against her inner thigh he raised her hand to his mouth. The tip of his tongue darted out in delicate strokes as he pressed his lips first against her fingertips then to the vulnerable white inside of her wrist.

"What are you doing?" Penny tried to laugh, for while it was obvious to her that his intentions were serious, his dark eyes held a glint of mischief.

"Trying to convince you," he said quietly.

"You're outdoing yourself," she mocked him gently. "Do you always go in for romance in public places?"

"Touché." He laughed and his warm breath tickled the inside of her wrist, sending a shiver of pleasure through her body. He flicked his tongue again as if to tease her into submission. There was, she thought, no need to convince her of anything. But she would not tell him that.

"I have a breakfast meeting with Max at seven." She laughed as he winced at the early hour.

She guessed by the devilish glint in his eyes that he was about to make some outlandishly suggestive retort, but before the words were out a piercing scream of recognition interrupted them and four well-dressed, middle-aged women appeared standing next to him.

"You're Buck!" the plumpest and most bejeweled of the lot exclaimed in a shrill soprano.

Joel glanced at the four women and smiled politely. "I *play* Buck."

"Look, it's Buck!" the plump lady announced proudly to the entire restaurant. She pounded Joel on the shoulder as if he were a stuffed dummy.

"We're sorry to interrupt you." A slender, dark-haired matron put a restraining arm on her fat friend.

"I knew it was you, Buck." The fat lady edged in on Joel with a broad, toothy smile that made Penny feel terribly embarrassed for her. The woman's three friends were clearly ill at ease in the situation.

"Are you his wife?" The fat lady threw Penny the question with all the subtlety of a big league pitcher.

"We were about to order dinner." Joel's voice was low, well modulated. Penny could see that he was doing his best to respond graciously to the pushy woman.

"Let's go, Elsie." The thin woman tugged on the fat lady's arm.

"Can we buy you a drink, Buck?" Elsie the Fat Lady pushed her face next to Joel's, and before he could reply, her gold braceleted arm was around his neck and her smudged, garnet lips were smooching his cheek. The other three women went pale with horror. Penny's spine went tense as she saw Joel stiffen and jump to his feet.

His eyes were blazing as he looked down on the presumptuous fan. "My name is Joel Sanborne," he said tersely and with much effort to control himself, "and not Buck Handlin. I am not public property."

Elsie's face turned redder, and she backed away from him before giving a self-conscious giggle. "Well, for heaven's sake. I was just paying you a compliment."

"I didn't hear any compliment." Joel glared at her. "I only heard a rude woman making a fool of herself."

Joel sat back down in his chair and his eyes sought Penny's with a desperate look. There was a moment's terrible silence before the fat woman recovered and let loose a barrage of insults. Who did he think he was? God? Penny listened rigidly as the woman railed against Joel for his snobbish, haughty, thankless attitude, and ended by saying that he owed his livelihood to people like her who condescended to watch his crappy show. Finally Elsie's three friends managed to drag her away, but her voice could be heard in the background harping and harping away about how dumb and insignificant actors really were.

"Let's get out of here." Joel threw down some money and bolted from the restaurant with Penny hurrying after him.

They walked in silence through the narrow streets and along the shore road until they reached Fort Sewall at the end of Front Street. Joel sat doggedly on the grassy slope above the spot where the Revolutionary War cannons had been placed to ward off the British. He sat with his knees drawn up to his chest and his long arms folded around them.

"I don't blame you," Penny said finally. "You tried to be nice to her."

He bobbed his head abruptly but continued to frown out across the violet-colored waters.

"I never really considered how . . . how difficult it must sometimes be to be someone famous." Penny sat down next to him and tried to get his attention by looking around and up at him.

"Hardly famous," he snapped without looking at her.

"You are. People recognize you," she added.

"It's all negative," he said broodingly, "and I'm sick of it. I want out. I've wanted out for some time, but after something like this . . ."

"But the other three women were decent," Penny offered.

"The point is"—Joel faced her tautly—"I am sick to death of Buck Handlin, sick to death of being identified with him. I'm sick of acting."

"I don't believe that." Penny felt an ambiguous need to comfort him, yet she did not completely understand what he was getting at.

"It's a rotten business," Joel said with a sigh, "and I've been one of the so-called lucky ones. At least I've made a good living as Buck Handlin. So maybe I don't have a right to complain.

70

Maybe that woman is right. Maybe I do belong to *them* . . . the people who pay the bills."

"You don't belong to them!" Penny sprang up on her knees. "That woman invaded your privacy. She grabbed you and kissed you . . . hard. She could have . . . given you whiplash."

Joel gave her a quick, perfunctory smile. "I know I want off the show. I think Marblehead may be my swan song. And then . . . I don't know. Maybe I'll get out of show business altogether!"

"But you're *good!*" Penny said emphatically. "Maybe you should break with your villainous Buck role, but you're far too talented to quit. You should be doing films, plays—"

"You're very naïve." Joel looked at her coolly.

"So what if I am?" She faced him.

"And I gather you're also very ambitious." There was a faint note of criticism in his voice.

"I am ambitious. I do want to direct. I think I'd be good at it." Penny frowned suddenly and wondered vaguely why it seemed they were on the verge of some new confrontation.

"Good doesn't mean you'll succeed," he said. "Good is no guarantee whatsoever. You've seen the crap they put on nighttime television. And movies? Not only are they making fewer movies, but unless you're a production freak and heavy into science fiction, monsters, or flaming headless bodies, you might find it hard to place your talents."

"You're really bitter," Penny observed softly. He shrugged. "You're too talented, too complex a man to limit yourself to Buck Handlin."

"How do you know that?" He faced her with a hostile thrust of his chin.

"I'm a good judge of people," Penny said boldly, and he shrugged again.

"So you are going to set the world on fire as a director and—"

"I didn't say 'set the world on fire,' " she interrupted him.

". . . and I"—he ignored the intrusion—"am about to leave the ranks. Sounds like a case of bad timing." He threw her a sardonic smile.

71

He stood up wearily, and as he turned to pull her to her feet they both turned at the sound of Max's voice calling out to them.

"Jesus" Max wiped his brow. "Nobody's around. The bartender back at the oceanside restaurant said he thought he'd seen you walking down this way."

Max paused to catch his breath. His usually pale, thin face was crimson. "Have you seen Tippy?"

"No." Joel seemed as alarmed as Max.

"You?" Max glanced quickly at Penny and she shook her head.

"Was she feeling badly again?" Joel's solicitous attitude gave Penny an unwanted pang of jealousy.

"I don't know," Max said worriedly. "She always says she feels fine and then . . . whammo. I can't trust what she says. I've been phoning her room and there's no answer."

"Maybe she went for a swim," Penny offered, feeling suddenly awkward and out of place.

"No," Max barked. "Listen"—he zeroed in on Penny with a tense smile—"we have to talk about a few things. You've got to spend more time tightening these scripts. I'm not talking major changes, nothing you have to phone New York about. We're not up here to play, you know."

Max's unexpected rebuke turned her ashen. He had never spoken to her like that before, He usually had nothing but praise for the way she did her job.

"Take it easy, Max." Joel patted Max's shoulder. "Penny didn't do anything and you know it. I'll come with you and we'll see if we can track Tippy down."

Joel turned to Penny with a grim smile. "You can get back to the Club on your own?"

"Sure," Penny said and nodded. She was still reeling from Max's rebuke. Joel's defense seemed inadequate, and tears of frustration sprang to her eyes as the two men trotted off in search of Tippy Malone.

72

# CHAPTER FIVE

"All right," Max shouted as he squatted next to Serge Moarliski, who was working briefly with a hand-held camera. "Tippy, take that entrance again. I want you to open the back door slowly, very slowly, and then take your time meandering down the garden path to the grape arbor. Remember, you know Buck is out there waiting for you. You've seen him from your window, but you want to appear casual. You want him to think you've just come out for a little stroll."

Tippy nodded with the same vacant expression that came over her face whenever the cameras weren't rolling. Penny nudged Faye and asked her to powder down Tippy's face again before they started the scene. It was midafternoon, and the sun was beating down on the formal rose garden that was in the rear of the mansion.

"Take Tippy another glass of ice water," Penny whispered to a lanky young college student, a local fellow who had been hired to run errands for the production crew. She moved to one of the few shady areas and sat down gingerly on the grass, her sunburned legs stretched out in front of her. How stupid to have worn shorts today of all days. There were large red rings around her knees, blotches of red on her thighs, and the rest of her legs

73

were as white as chalk. She shoved her sunglasses to the top of her head and studied the freckles that had popped out on her arms. No doubt her nose was also liberally sprinkled with the noxious little dots. Shoving the dark glasses back down on her nose she watched as Joel, who was leaning solicitously over Tippy, motioned for Max. Joel and Max had been hovering over Tippy since ten that morning when they had begun shooting. The cast and crew were tense and irritable, not only because of the grueling heat but because of the growing concern over Tippy and the uncertainty as to whether or not she would make it through the day. Scenes had been switched to accommodate Tippy, and for some actors, Archie in particular, it was no easy job learning lines at the last minute.

Penny shuffled through some sheets on her clipboard and made a note that Tippy had added a white hankie to her costume. They would need to know that detail when they matched shots for the same scene later on.

"I have to talk to you." Archie Marshall stood over Penny, frowning.

"They're getting ready to roll," Penny whispered, but Archie motioned her away and she followed him off to the right of the rose garden to where a small greenhouse was situated. Penny cautioned herself to relax. She could see Archie had something discomforting on his mind.

"I can't say these lines." He shoved the script angrily at her.

"Archie, we're set up for this scene next. I don't see how we can make any changes at this late stage." Penny's voice remained calm despite the fact that Archie was shaking his head in disdain.

"Look, Max and I did our best to trim out some of that awkward dialogue. Just like you asked us to do but—"

"It's not enough," Archie interrupted.

"You know I can't take time to phone New York now," she said patiently. "Please, go with this and I promise you if you have problems with the scenes set for tomorrow I will personally try to convince Max to get more substantial rewrites from the writers."

"What a mess," Archie griped, but before he could continue his tirade Max screamed out for Penny, and she took off running back across the grass to where the action was.

"Where have you been?" Max barked irritably. "Why don't you stay where you're supposed to be?"

"Sorry." Penny bit back an explanation. Max had enough on his mind without contending with Archie's niggling problems.

"We're breaking for an hour," Max directed, "then we'll do the scene with Irene and Archie. If we finish that before the light goes we'll pick up some exteriors out front."

"Right." Penny jotted a few notes. "Did you get a good take on the last scene?"

But Max was already hurrying toward Tippy, who was leaning languidly against Joel. Penny turned away more perturbed than upset. There had not been much of an opportunity to talk to Joel because both of them had been working constantly since morning. Several times he had sought her out, but she had managed to find some reason to rush off. His concern about Tippy had tipped the balance of her objective emotional equilibrium. All day she had simply been trying not to think. She just wanted to do her work.

"I'm bushed." Irene kicked off her white spike heels and collapsed in the grass next to Penny. "Waiting is so exhausting."

"So is running dumb errands." Penny smiled sarcastically. "You'll get grass stain on your dress."

Irene grimaced and jumped up, brushing frantically at her full-skirted pink dress with its revealing low neckline. "I can't even sit down!"

"Them's the breaks," Penny teased, but her smile faded and her stomach flipped in nervous anticipation as she saw Joel walking slowly toward her. He had changed out of his work clothes and looked crisp and cool in white tennis shorts and a lime green T-shirt.

"Tennis anyone?" He mimicked a fierce forehand.

"Don't I wish," lamented Irene as she bent over and retrieved her high-heeled shoes. "See you two later."

Joel smiled down at Penny. Clearly he had recovered from yesterday's incident in the restaurant. "How about dinner?" he asked casually.

Penny's stomach tightened, and for the first time since he and Max had rushed off in search of Tippy she realized how angry she was. She had revealed so much of herself to him yesterday and then he'd left so suddenly without even a phone call later on to explain what had happened.

"I don't have any idea what time we'll be finished here." She forced her voice to remain calm even though her stomach was churning.

"I'll wait." He brushed a wisp of hair off her forehead.

"That's nice of you," she said with a smile, but her voice sounded formal and stiff, "but I have tons of . . . homework. I've had a lot of complaints about the scripts."

It wasn't a total lie, she thought. A flicker of resentment crossed Joel's face. She knew by now how difficult it was for him to handle rejection, and part of her reveled in his momentary discomfort. Part of her wanted to hurt him as he had hurt her by leaving her so abruptly last night.

"You have to eat." He gave her one of his most charming smiles.

"In my room." She faked a playful shrug. "I've done it before. Tuna on rye bread with wilted lettuce. Really . . . I'm exhausted. I think I should leave myself clear."

Joel picked up his imaginary tennis racket and gave a feeble whack at an imaginary ball. They both laughed as if they thought it was funny. "I struck out." Joel grinned as if her rejection was of no consequence. "See you later."

Much later that night Penny let herself into her room and fell on her bed in a numbed state of exhaustion. She squinted at the little digital travel clock and wondered vaguely how she had been stupid enough to go to dinner with Pierre Fabre, the New York public relations man who was covering the shoot. At first it had seemed like a good idea. Pierre was charming; she'd met him a

76

couple of times in New York, and he had indulged her by tolerating her somewhat halting French, which she spoke almost exclusively in the present tense.

Penny kicked off the strappy white sandals with the French heels and struggled to her feet to remove her red and white cotton pinafore. What had she been trying to prove by going to dinner with Pierre, drinking two martinis when she never drank anything but white wine? And then, as luck would have it, Joel had come into the restaurant alone and seen her dining with Pierre. Penny winced again. Her earlier sense of triumph had ebbed along with her martini high. It was time to face facts. She had behaved stupidly, spending an evening with one man when she had been dying to spend it with another.

"Damn!" She stood in the middle of her room in her panties and bra, and gazed down at her blotched, sunburned legs feeling stupid, unattractive, and hopeless. She padded across her room and threw open the French doors, letting the cool sea breeze flow over her warm body. Through the trellis that separated her terrace from Joel's she could see that there was a light on in his room. So close, she thought, so close. She sat down at the table for a few minutes and then glided back across the terrace to stand next to the trellis.

Her mouth was parched and stale-tasting from the martinis. "Joel . . ." she called softly. "Are you there?"

She held her breath waiting, and her body tingled with irrational desire. Dimly she knew this to be extraordinary behavior on her part. She felt positively wild and her heart was thundering. It occurred to her that he would hurtle the trellis and clasp her nearly naked body to his. She could almost feel his hands removing her lacy bra, feel his moist hot breath on her breasts. . . .

"Joel . . . ?" She was behaving foolishly. She imagined if only he would answer, if only he would understand that she had gone out with Pierre because she had been hurt, there would be no reason for them not to make love.

Suddenly his side of the terrace was plunged into darkness,

and moments later she heard, or thought she heard, the low rumble of his Porsche speeding off into the night. Penny gazed up at the starry sky, haunted by the feeling that her phony pride had ruined everything. He had asked her to dinner; she had rejected him. She stripped out of the panties and bra, and walked naked back into her room. How long had it been since she had cried, really cried? She slid under the covers and her cheeks were damp with hot summer tears. And she could not say *he* had made her miserable. It was all, all of it, her own doing.

Her sleep was predictably restless, and she wakened the next morning before the alarm sounded. She padded into the bathroom and stood under an icy shower, shaved her legs, which were now miraculously a healthy brown, and after drying herself with one of the large, nubby white towels, smoothed a sweet, orange-scented lotion all over her body. She dressed carefully in crisp white shorts which hit her just above the knees and a matching white shirt. By the time the bellboy had set up her coffee and grapefruit on the terrace she was feeling a bit more optimistic about her prospects. She would, of course, apologize to him, and he, being the sensible man she knew him to be, would accept. It was simple. Last night she had been so tired that her imagination had created horror where none existed. After all, they were intelligent, rational people, not neurotic, driven characters in a soap opera.

Penny sipped the hot coffee, luxuriating in the extra time. She went through the day's scripts and made a few changes, all the while listening for signs of life from Joel's room. Finally at eight o'clock she let herself out of her room, planning to walk to the location. She wasn't due there until nine thirty, so there would be plenty of time. She passed the swimming pool as Joel, looking cross and unshaven, was climbing out.

"You're ambitious." She waved and smiled, but he did not respond. He picked up his towel and rubbed his dark hair furiously.

"I'm sorry about last night." Penny crossed to him quickly. "I shouldn't have accepted Pierre's invitation after I—"

78

"It's your business if you want to have dinner with Pierre."

"I didn't want to—" she began.

"Then it was a dumb thing to do, wasn't it?" Joel eyed her harshly.

"Yes," she admitted ruefully, "it was *really* dumb."

He looked off as if something else was on his mind, then quickly back at Penny as if he had forgotten she was there. "I'd better get dressed or I'll be late for work. See you on the set."

And that, thought Penny as she walked along the road toward the old mansion, is why one should never mix business with pleasure. As she rounded the final curve of the road Irene pedaled up beside her on a rusty bike.

"I rented it for the rest of the time," Irene announced breathlessly. "It's good for your thighs."

"For *your* thighs," Penny said and smiled. "I'm too nervous to ride on the road. I'm strictly a sidewalk biker."

Irene hopped off the bike and walked alongside Penny. "You seem sad," the blonde observed after a few moments.

Penny glanced at her quizzically. "Am I that transparent?"

"Not usually," Irene admitted. "Also, you're all dressed up. Usually you wear jeans or old ratty clothes to work up here. Something happen between you and Joel?"

"Irene!" Penny exploded, then she shook her head, sighing. "You're right. I'm miserable. Max is on my back every minute. I can't seem to do anything right . . ."

"And Joel?" Irene inquired softly.

"I . . . I really like him," Penny confessed hesitantly. "It's like I'm not myself though . . . or maybe it's just too complicated trying to work and . . . I don't know." She broke off exasperated, and they walked a few minutes in silence.

"I think I'm letting my emotions get in the way of my work," Penny said finally. "I can't help myself. I thought I was able to handle seeing Tippy and Joel do those love scenes, but I find myself resenting her."

"That must be weird," Irene observed sympathetically.

Joel's Porsche whizzed past them with Tippy in the front seat. Irene and Penny exchanged looks.

"He just offered her a ride," Irene said reassuringly, but Penny was not convinced, and throughout the day, which was as tense and unrewarding as the day before, Penny fought off feelings of depression as Joel continued to hover around Tippy.

Disaster after disaster strained everyone's tempers: a broken cable; a minor feud between Archie and Joel; several misplaced props on Tippy's part. Because they were running so far behind, Max elected to go into overtime, which of course meant a massive increase in costs. Not surprisingly the work Penny had done on the scripts did not please Archie, and consequently Max was even more irritated with her than he'd been yesterday. Joel steered clear of her.

By six the light was nearly gone, but Max was determined to make it through the scene that was set in the grape arbor: a passionate scene in which Joel was to convince Tippy to run away with him.

Penny, standing to one side with lowered eyes, tried not to watch as Joel pressed his body against Tippy's. When Max called "Cut," Archie, who had been standing next to Penny, gave a low chuckle.

"Damn Joel is up to it again." Archie shook his head admiringly.

Penny started to inch away, but Archie seemed inclined to talk. "I think the old spark has come alive." He caught her eye, then nodded toward the arbor where Max was giving the two stars some additional direction.

"Maybe so," Penny said wearily.

"Oh yes." Archie reached in his jacket for a cigarette and offered one to Penny, which she declined. "They used to be quite an item."

"So I've heard." Penny took in a quick breath.

"They weren't acting that time around," Archie mused, and Penny bit back an insult. How could he tell they weren't acting?

She moved away from Archie, feeling a headache begin to

80

throb. Of course he had just been needling her. There was no way he could tell that they weren't acting. She moved down the slope toward the greenhouse and stood by herself until Max shouted for her. He was going to do one more take for close-ups, and if it went well he would move right on to the scene where Archie would discover that Tippy, who played his wife, had left with his archenemy Buck Handlin.

Penny armed herself for another "viewing" as Joel began to caress Tippy's pale, slender neck. His hands traveled down the side of her body. Did they linger too long?

Then suddenly everyone was screaming and Max was shouting hysterically for someone to call a doctor. Tippy lay limp in Joel's arms, and her face was ashen.

"Tippy . . . baby . . . come on . . ." Joel urged, leaning over her. He rubbed his cheek against hers and very gently lowered her to the ground where he continued to crouch over her.

Penny turned away overcome with confusion over the complexity of her feelings. Perhaps Archie had not been lying after all. Joel's concern seemed to go a long way toward supporting Archie's contention. But how could she be thinking such niggardly, petty thoughts when Tippy was obviously quite ill?

"Penny!" Max pulled on her arm in a frenzy. "I'm going with Tippy—I'm taking her to a doctor. Okay? You take over. You have plenty of time to finish Archie's bit. Go mostly for close-ups . . . you know. You'll be fine!"

Max rushed off in a panic. Those were the first kind words of encouragement that Max had uttered to her all week. Penny paused to consider the possibilities. This was an incredible break. True, it was a brief scene, but it was crucial to the segment and highly dramatic. If she pulled it off well it would be a dynamic piece of film, a clip that might lead to something big.

First she called the crew together explaining that they would be jumping ahead to Archie's scene. They would take fifteen minutes to set up and start shooting immediately. Everyone was behind her; she could feel the ranks falling together the way they usually did in an emergency. She moved back down the hill to study the script and make some quick decisions about shots. Her mind switched smoothly into creative overdrive. All thoughts of Joel disappeared, and for the next fifteen minutes she was totally concentrated on the task ahead. Finally she conferred with Serge on several of the camera angles, and then they were ready to go. As she approached Archie to give him some of her directorial observations, she felt confident. It was the sort of scene that Archie did best, so she could quite honestly give him the sort of support he usually needed. However, before she could open her mouth, a slow smile on his face stopped her cold.

"I can't go with this," he said sanguinely.

"What do you mean?" Penny asked briskly, wanting to appear firm and unruffled.

"This is one of the few decent scenes I have and I'm damned if I'll let an amateur direct it."

Penny blanched. "I don't believe you said that to me, Archie."

"You better believe it." Archie met her eyes with an insipid smile that turned her stomach.

"I'm hardly an amateur," Penny ventured then wished she hadn't stooped to defending her position. In point of fact, he had no choice. She was the director; he was the actor. He had to do the scene.

"All right," Penny shouted, "let's roll with it." She moved out of focus to assume her position next to Serge and as she did, Archie did the unthinkable—he walked out of the frame and off the premises.

Penny was stunned. A hush of disbelief fell over the crew and the remaining actors. Penny felt a hand on her shoulder and turned to see quiet, bespectacled Serge offering his condolences.

"That bastard," said Serge, who never had an ill thing to say about anybody.

Penny shook her head. Never in her life had she felt so humiliated, never felt like such a failure. She fought back her tears, fought back the impulse to run after Archie and beg him to come back . . . or to engage him in battle . . . anything. After a moment she turned to the crew and without acknowledging Archie's unprofessional behavior announced that they would do some pickup shots of Irene.

Wordlessly the crew went to work, every eye admiring Penny's ability to continue after such a disgusting display of temperament. Irene put her arm around Penny and hugged her.

Penny directed the segments efficiently . . . there was really nothing to it, certainly very little challenge. Afterward, without exception, everyone in the crew came forward to congratulate her. She smiled despite her aching disappointment; she knew she had at least gained something . . . the respect of the crew. It was not something to be taken lightly.

As she gathered up her canvas bag of scripts she looked around hopefully on the off chance that Joel had waited for her, but no. . . . On the way in to town with Serge and Tom, who were taking her for a beer, Serge mentioned that Joel had also gone to the doctor's with Tippy.

# CHAPTER SIX

Penny slid down into the hot foamy bathwater, and for what felt like the zillionth time told herself that the breach which had developed in her relationship with Joel was really for the best. Another day had passed since Tippy had fainted, since Archie Marshall had tried to humiliate her by walking off the set. A day that had at least proved more productive workwise. There had been no more ambiguous fainting spells on Tippy's part, no more tantrums from Archie. And Joel?

Penny stretched one long, nicely tanned leg out of the water and began to shave it carefully. Joel was congenial, he smiled at her, once he had even brought her a container of iced tea. But it was not the same. Clearly he too had arrived at some decision about the advisability of—Penny winced at the phrase but there was none other—"getting involved."

She told herself it was a relief and it made things sadder but easier. She now had days of gray constancy rather than black lows and crimson highs. Tomorrow was their first day off since arriving in Marblehead and in one hour, at seven o'clock, the entire *Dream of Life* cast and crew were being entertained on board the *Luscious*.

The *Luscious*, according to Pierre, was a *"très yare"* sixty-

three-foot ketch in which the owner, a salty young Boston banker, had sailed across the Atlantic four times. They would be
filming the denouement on board the splendid vessel at the end
of the week. Penny smiled, recalling the conversation between
herself, Pierre, and Irene that had taken place earlier. Irene had
commented with a perfectly straight face that she cared neither
for "yare" nor "ketch" . . . all she cared about was that the
banker who owned it was *young.* Now that she was getting to
know Irene, Penny could see a wonderfully original comedic
quality in her. Perhaps when they got back to New York she
would scrape together some money and shoot a very, *very* short
audition tape with her.

Ah, plans, plans. Penny wiped off the steamy mirror and, her
body still glistening with water, began to apply a touch of makeup. She and Irene had both purchased new bikinis for the occasion. After she toweled off, she slipped on the brief yellow suit
and over it a loose-fitting Indian caftan. It was likely to be a very
late night, but that was the least of her worries. If need be she
would spend Sunday sleeping.

There was a tap on her door as Irene and Pierre urged Penny
to hurry or they would literally miss the boat.

"We're sailing up the coast to Beverly." Irene yakked excited-
ly as she twisted around in the front seat of Pierre's convertible.
"I've never been on a boat before!"

"It might make you green, *ma petite.*" Pierre jabbed Irene
playfully, a gesture that confirmed what Penny had been suspect-
ing for several days. Dear, quiet, sweet Pierre had quite a crush
on Irene. Seeing Irene's flustered response at his gesture, Penny
guessed that Irene reciprocated those feelings.

Suddenly Penny felt overcome with loneliness. Oh, she was
happy for Irene and Pierre, they were two of her favorite people,
but seeing the excitement in their eyes when they looked at each
other made her more aware than ever of the loss she felt. And
that was stupid. She had no business feeling anything after
spending only three evenings with Joel . . . and not quite three
because of the interruption from Max. Two and a half evenings

with Joel Sanborne. Well, she was glad he wasn't coming this evening. She had overheard him telling Tippy that he thought he would drive back to New York City immediately after work, leave his car there, and then fly back to Marblehead in time for work Monday morning. The knowledge that he wouldn't be around for the next day should have been a relief . . . but it wasn't.

The *Luscious* was only one of many illustrious, gleaming white sailing vessels that were moored at the marina, but they all agreed it was the most majestic. On board there was all the sophisticated bustle of a chic New York cocktail party. An excellent stereo system filled the air with Oscar Peterson's piano music as white-coated butlers passed trays of exotic hors d'oeuvres.

"That's why I call her the *Luscious,*" the young Boston banker, Ross Herrington, proclaimed. He was a plump, balding little man in his early thirties, and he greeted the three newcomers enthusiastically, immediately zeroing in on petite Irene. But his Bostonian sense of decorum prevailed, and when he quickly sensed the rapport between Irene and Pierre he switched his good-natured enthusiasm to Penny and whisked her off to introduce her to the rest of his Boston friends.

As the yacht pulled out of the Marblehead marina Penny found herself in the midst of what was obviously a very jet-set, yachting crowd. It was Palm Beach this, Paris and Zürich that, and what is the water temperature in Bar Harbor this time of year? Suddenly Joel's deep baritone cut through the clamor of conversation, and Penny whirled around to see him surrounded by a bevy of deeply tanned Bostonian beauties. The knowledge that he had not driven back to New York sent her into a tailspin despite her earlier conclusion, and her heart was racing. For the first time all evening she felt alive. The mere sound of his voice had set off a visceral reaction. Suddenly her conversation was more animated, there was laughter where there had been none. The world was sharp, in focus.

For the next hour she laughed and drank with Ross Herrington and several of his friends. Once she caught Joel staring at her, but he only gave her a quick hello then looked away. Now the *Luscious* was about to put down anchor in a little cove outside of Beverly so that those who wanted to indulge in a swim under the waxing moon could do so. Memories of her moonlight swim with Joel infused her with a fierce craving so that when she slipped out of the caftan and stood on the prow of the yacht in her new bikini she felt almost dizzy.

The air was filled with laughter and splashing as the guests climbed down the rope ladder and plunged into the dark, velvety waters. In the spirit of abandon Penny made a clean dive into the salty water and joined in a game of water ball with some of her new acquaintances and several members of the crew. Through the clamor she listened for the sound of Joel's voice, hoping that he would enter the game.

Ross had hung several lanterns off the prow so there was a minimal amount of light. Above her she heard someone call for "lights out so we can get down to some serious skinny-dipping." The laughter seemed to crescendo then, and Penny was aware that most of the people around her were removing their swimming suits and hurling them back onto the *Luscious*. Quietly she swam over to the boat and climbed back up the ladder just in time to see Joel, clad in the well-remembered navy trunks, popping an hors d'oeuvre into the mouth of a very beautiful woman. Penny turned away as he laughed. She moved into the shadows and waited until she heard several loud splashes, then thinking he had dived off the boat, she turned to go down into the galley and dress.

She took in a quick breath at the unexpected sight of Joel's naked body as he stood with his back to her, poised and ready to dive. Suddenly he disappeared over the side of the boat, and a loud chorus of female voices cheered his daring.

Penny threw a towel around her shoulders and sat huddled on the starboard side of the boat. Despite the awkwardness of the situation, she could not shake the raging desire she felt for Joel. She guessed by the sound of his voice and the heaviness in his laugh that he had had a lot to drink. Well, so had they all, herself included. But the swim had sobered her somewhat and all she wanted now was a hot cup of coffee which she knew she would find in the galley. She dripped her way along the deck, pausing to speak briefly to Max and Tippy, who had not donned swimming suits.

The galley was deserted, or so she believed until she noticed Irene scrunched into a corner leafing listlessly through a *National Geographic*.

"You're not swimming?" Penny asked as she poured herself a cup of coffee.

"I can't take my clothes off," Irene admitted with a tragic expression.

"So swim in your suit," Penny advised. "I did. There are people up there in their suits."

Irene grimaced and looked as if she were about to be sick. "I've never been to a party like this," she said. "I feel really out of it."

"Irene!" Penny's laugh bordered on nervous tears as she moved to embrace the younger woman.

"I guess I'm too conventional." Irene shook her head. "Maybe I have sexual hangups."

"Maybe," said Penny, "you just don't want to go skinny-dipping. Don't feel guilty about it."

"I guess maybe I will." Irene stood up, and after a moment she smiled at Penny and left the galley.

Penny finished her coffee and wandered around the main cabin trying to find her caftan. As soon as everyone finished swimming the *Luscious* would sail on into Beverly, where caterers were bringing on board a full midnight supper. Max had had someone drive his car to Beverly in case Tippy did not feel like making the sail back to Marblehead. Perhaps she would join them. There seemed little point in staying for the final leg of the sail.

She heard someone climb down the hatch but did not turn around until the only light in the cabin was turned off.

"Who's there?" As she squinted to adjust to the darkness she felt cool wet hands on her bare shoulders. Her stomach stirred and her whole body shuddered as she recognized Joel's large sensitive fingers massaging the soft skin of her shoulders. With a sense of disbelief Penny surrendered to his expert touch, feeling the tension drain from her tired muscles. Words were beyond her; it seemed to be enough that he had sought her out. She shut her eyes, luxuriating in the pressure his hand was exerting on her bare back as he rubbed and prodded along her spine. As he moved closer she prepared herself for the full impact of his nakedness. When she felt his damp legs push against hers from behind her own legs buckled slightly, and she swayed involuntarily as his cool lips grazed the nape of her neck. He showered light, summer-hot kisses on her neck and moved gracefully around to face her.

"Penny . . . my Penny," he breathed into her ear, and she felt mesmerized by his presence. Unable to control her curiosity she lowered her eyes briefly. He had put the tight navy swimming trunks back on. A shaky smile crossed her face at this token of propriety.

"I've wanted to talk to you all evening . . ." He lifted her chin up, and she faced him squarely.

"I've wanted to talk to you too." Penny's voice was barely a whisper.

Joel reached for her hand, gave it a long squeeze, and then guided it to his naked chest. Instantly she yielded to the intense pleasure his cool skin brought to her. Her hand was shaking as she moved it slowly around his chest, testing the wiry hairs, familiarizing herself with the texture of his skin and with his rib cage, which seemed amazingly fragile beneath her touch. His breathing accelerated as she dared to take one small hard nipple in her mouth and hold it lightly between her teeth. Unable to contain himself Joel lifted her face to his and brought his mouth down firmly on hers. She gasped, not in protest but with excruciating pleasure as he eased his tongue into her eager mouth.

Then she felt his hand firmly on her waist guiding her through the darkened main cabin toward what she sensed was the aft cabin. She allowed him to propel her along, occasionally feeling his cool hairy legs brush against her smooth calves. She closed her eyes against the darkness of this unfamiliar space, amazed that this was happening and that she trusted him to steer her safely past all obstacles. Her own breathing was coming in shallow gasps. She knew precisely what was happening, and her lithe body quivered in anticipation. She was glad she had not had that much to drink. She wanted her senses to be alive to his every touch. Recalling the taste of his mouth on hers, she guessed that he too had been pacing himself. And all along she had thought he was drinking heavily. Had he had this moment in mind all evening? Had he only been waiting for the opportunity?

"Ouch . . ." His hand left her waist, and in the dim light she could see him hopping on one foot and holding his toe.

"Are you okay?" She pressed against him solicitously, but her nearness banished his momentary pain and his answer was to take her in his arms and kiss her again.

The fervor of his kiss took her breath away, and when they finally reached the door to the aft cabin she could scarcely walk. Her hand continued to caress his torso as he opened the door, closed it behind them, locked it, and lowered her to the narrow bed.

Penny looked up at his face expectantly. Now that her eyes had grown accustomed to the dark, it was possible to make out his expression. A new shiver of anticipation swept over her as she read the hungry desire in his eyes. He stared at her prone body clad only in the brief swimming suit, and she flexed the muscles in her thighs as if to ward off the excess of wild abandon she was experiencing. She lay very still with her arms at her sides allowing him to feast his eyes for as long as he liked, and although he made no move to remove her flimsy suit, she felt herself already bared to him.

"The porthole . . ." A slender shaft of light crossed the foot of the bed. She had not noticed it at first, but as Joel bent to remove his suit it cut across his smooth, tanned back. He rose slowly in all of his splendor, and Penny's lips parted in a hushed gasp. He was the most beautiful man. . . . She could not tear her eyes away from the full sight of him as he crouched over her and reached out to cut off the light that was spilling in from the porthole. Her hands sought him impatiently and drew him down onto her. The familiar weight ignited her. She was ravenous and suddenly even a moment's hesitation was unbearable. They had waited long enough and she was unleashed. Her need for him was devastating.

Their breathing was mixed and ragged as he moved to one side, drew her into a sitting position and skillfully untied the top of her new bikini.

"I like it." He nibbled at the middle of her back then as her bikini top fell from her body he reached around her and cupped her breasts in his hands. She leaned against his chest and tried not to cry out in joy and passion.

But the touch of his hands could no longer satisfy her, and again the wild desire overtook her and she shifted around to face him, pressing her breasts against his chest and seeking his warm mouth. She felt herself surging in to him, imparting her own heated impatience to him.

She was in a near frenzy when he pulled away from her and took one hard pink nipple into his wet, cool mouth. His tongue made maddening circles around the nipple while his hands, inflamed and urged on by her undulating body, slid down her silken torso until they reached the elastic top of her bikini bottoms.

He slid one finger underneath the elastic and then abruptly stopped moving. Penny tried to clasp him closer, but he raised himself above her and studied her with a searching, expression. "I am . . . sorry . . ." He forced the words out.

"Sorry . . . ?" Penny, so near to exploding, felt the chill of confusion sweep over her.

"For behaving so childishly these past two days." Joel lowered his full weight back onto her and began nuzzling her neck.

"I've behaved foolishly . . ." Penny twisted her head and found his mouth. She felt as if her entire being were directed toward him in that kiss. There was nothing she did not want from this man. She wanted everything!

"Let's not"—Joel paused to suck in some air—"ever behave foolishly again."

"No"—Penny wrapped her arms around his lean hard body—"let's not."

"Ever. . . . Let's not *ever,*" Joel growled as his hands inched the bikini bottoms over her hips.

Penny let out a muffled cry as Joel's hands paved the way for that ultimate moment she craved. Her taut stomach was a field for his foraging tongue; then when it seemed she could no longer endure the torment of his lavish prelude he burst in on her, plunging into her very soul with lightning-smooth strokes.

Every crevice of her body came alive as the bounteous power of his manhood erupted. He gripped her hips exuberantly, leading her into new and varied rhythms that sent waves of ecstasy crashing inside of her. She was breathless, her skin as wet as if she had emerged from beneath the ocean's surface. The motion of his body elicited undreamed of responses, and in a state of near frenzy she thought it was nothing short of wondrous that he should know so much about her to bring her again and again to such shattering heights of fulfillment.

They clasped at each other as if there would never be enough time, and their bodies, once cool from the ocean's waters, emitted a damp warmth. His lips upon her eyelids were as gentle, as soft, as the velvety petals of a summer rose. And yet again he held himself off, offering her limitless pleasure, smiling softly as she soared from peak to peak.

The music and laughter outside the cabin had long since dimmed and faded into oblivion. The only life existed within, in the thick darkness that was filled with the hushed vibrations of their lovemaking.

Penny stretched beneath his slick hot body, and her every movement seemed to be anticipated by Joel. He was, she thought, inside her mind, for he seemed to know what was needed, and how and when. When he finally took the moment for himself a new power coursed through her body, for as he shook and trembled in her arms she knew that she had led him to this final sublime explosion.

At last they lay clasped in each other's arms as if nothing would ever part them. The silence surrounding them now was complete, and nestling against each other in the little cabin, they wore twin smiles. It seemed to Penny that they might sail on and on forever on a sea as calm as the desires they evoked from each other were tumultuous and unpredictable. The tiny compartment had offered them a rare respite. Penny closed her eyes, relishing the erotic sensations still dancing in her body. Joel took her hand, raised it to his lips, and kissed it.

"Where do you suppose we are?" Penny murmured after a while when she felt the *Luscious* begin to glide through the waters.

"Do you care?" Joel stroked her face and bent to kiss her lightly on the lips.

"No," she said, smiling at him, and it was true. She cared for nothing except knowing that they were together. She cared for nothing except the light in his eyes which told her all she needed to know. She chuckled softly as she snuggled into his arms.

"What is it?" he asked softly.

"I hope whoever is staying in this cabin doesn't decide to retire early from the celebration."

"When you know me better," breathed Joel, "you will know that I am not the impromptu person I appear to be. Do you think I would have steered you into a stranger's cabin?"

Penny squinted at him. He was grinning at her like the Cheshire cat. "You devil," she teased. "This is your cabin? You were invited to stay on board?"

"Buck Handlin was invited," Joel whispered, and they both giggled like children who were conspiring.

"And who are you now?" Penny said half joking.

Joel's dark eyes grew serious, and he paused for some time studying her face as if he could read the future in it. "I am Joel

Sanborne. . . . I have never been more Joel Sanborne than I am this minute."

As Penny drew his face down to hers there were tears of happiness in her eyes. Joel Sanborne was a rare man . . . and she? At the moment she knew herself to be the luckiest woman in the world.

# CHAPTER SEVEN

By the time the *Luscious* pulled alongside of the dock in Beverly, Joel and Penny had drifted back up onto the deck to join the rest of the party. Beneath the soft folds of her blue and white caftan her body tingled with a new awareness. As she walked toward the prow of the boat with her fingers laced in Joel's she neither knew nor cared if anyone had missed them. With her damp hair pulled back from her face and fastened with a large barrette, Penny's face glowed.

"I'm going to make excuses to Ross," Joel said when they were standing alone. "I'll tell him I got a touch queasy on the way up and that we'll drive back to Marblehead with either Max or Serge."

"You'd do that for me?" Penny teased lightly, but she felt a ripple of pleasure knowing that Joel preferred being with her to a night and a day on the sea on Ross Herrington's luxurious yacht.

"And that's not all I'll do for you," Joel promised with an evil chuckle.

"I'm going to hold you to that," Penny retorted, and as he walked off in search of Ross she marveled at how easy and natural everything seemed between them. She looked off toward the lights of Beverly with a rapt smile. She was still amazed at what had transpired between them. So much about the way they were with each other surpassed her wildest dreams. Of course, even though she was intent on her career, she had from time to time thought about what kind of man she might want to spend the rest of her life with. A sense of humor had certainly always been at the top of her list of "qualifications"—she often felt herself bubbling up when she was with Joel. She'd also wanted a man with intelligence, sensitivity, consideration for others, and a sense of humanity—Joel had all of these. But there was something more, something she had never before been able to define for herself, and that too existed when she was with Joel. What she felt was an impelling need to make him happy—not to serve him or subordinate herself to him but to care for him in the very deepest sense. She cared about his happiness, and that caring had elevated their lovemaking to absolutely unimagined heights, for the desire to please him had reverted back to her a thousandfold.

And was this love? Penny smiled softly, raising her eyes to the starry August sky, to the milky moon whose right corner had a funny little gnawed-out portion missing. If love meant joyous exhilaration, caring deeply about the other person's happiness; if it meant wanting to share every image, including that gnawed-out corner of the moon; and if it meant wanting always to know that that one special person was there . . . then this was love. How odd then that she wasn't trembling with fear, with apprehension that things might not "work out." But maybe that was love too. At the moment she felt positively invincible, ravishingly beautiful, and, she giggled out loud, totally mad!

She glanced back over her shoulder to where Joel, with one arm thrown amicably around Ross Herrington's shoulder, was speaking intently. No doubt he was convincing Ross that it was seasickness and not lovesickness that was making him desert ship. Penny smiled as the two men approached her.

"Joel tells me you're feeling a little queasy," Ross sympathetically said.

Penny's mouth flew open, but before she could protest, Joel, who was standing a tad behind Ross, gave her a demented, moronic look which very nearly caused her to burst out laughing.

"Right." Penny quickly assumed a dour expression.

"I told Joel to take my car," Ross said. "I'm sorry you'll miss the supper."

"Oh," Penny said weakly, "food is the last thing on my mind." Joel caught her eye again and smacked his lips with a tantalizing smile.

"It's been wonderful though, Ross. Really a wonderful . . ." Penny paused, actually to keep from laughing. She coughed to cover her response. ". . . wonderful sail. It's been a wonderful sail, Ross."

Ross patted her on the back. "Anytime," he said. "You and Joel are welcome on board the *Luscious* anytime."

"Nice of you." Joel shook the young banker's hand. "I'll leave the car keys with the guard at the marina."

Ross nodded unsuspectingly. "If you're up to it around noon tomorrow I think we'll take her out again for an afternoon sail. Maybe stop up Gloucester way for some lobster."

As soon as they were out of sight of the *Luscious,* Joel and Penny collapsed in each other's arms, laughing.

"I might have known," Penny said with a mocking glare, "that you would shift the blame to me. Didn't want to ruin your image, is that it?"

Joel doubled over, laughing. "I didn't care about my image," he said. "I just wanted to catch you off guard. You should have seen your face!"

Penny punched him playfully on the arm. "You should have seen *your* face. I think you missed your calling. I'm not sure you wouldn't make a better clown than you do a villain."

"Ho ho ho." Joel swung her off the ground and landed a wet kiss on her lips.

The parking lot was deserted, and they walked with their arms wrapped around each other until they located Ross's sleek, silver Jaguar convertible.

"With the wind in your hair"—Joel opened the door for Penny—"you will be even more beautiful."

Before Penny could step inside the car he took her in his arms and, pressing her up against the car, rubbed his body against hers. "All that talk of midnight suppers. Like you, food is about the last thing on my mind."

He nibbled at her ear, then locking his arms around her, they swayed in the moonlight until the fires that raged in Penny made her feel faint.

"I can't stop." Joel's passionate response stirred against her. Small warm bumps sprang out along her arm when she felt his lips brush against her neck.

"You don't have to." Penny's voice was husky as she crushed her curves against his hard, undulating body.

"I never want to stop kissing you." His mouth sought hers again, and she yielded to his tender, stroking tongue moving in and out of her moist and eager lips. The memory of their lovemaking was so near the surface that the sensation of his tongue brought on a new wave of desire. She flushed and flicked her tongue along his lips.

"What shall we do?" He held her away from him, panting hungrily.

"You're asking me?" Penny half laughed in spite of the almost excrutiating desire raging with her. Joel touched her breast tentatively, looked around, and then when he was sure they were alone, bent to kiss it lightly.

"Are we crazy?" Joel pulled her back against him again and clutched her tightly as if that were the only way he could still his roaming hands.

"I think so." Penny's hands moved from his back to his chest. Through the thin silk of his shirt she tested the wiry hairs of his firm chest. She closed her eyes, moving her hands more slowly, then she pressed her cheek to him. It seemed that the imprint of his body lived in her mind. She moved her hands brazenly to his belt buckle and felt him stir against her.

"We've got to get back to Marblehead," Joel murmured. "And somebody has to drive."

"I'm seasick," Penny replied drowsily. "I guess it'll have to be you." She removed her hands and gave him a prudent little grin.

There was a magical closeness between them as they drove back to Marblehead. Joel spoke of his youth in Chicago, and Penny introduced him to members of her family back in Virginia. They shared secrets and compared aspects of their pasts, devouring the details of each other's lives as passionately and eagerly as their bodies had met earlier.

"I hate stick shifts," Penny complained, wanting to snuggle against him. She put her hand on his hard thigh and caressed it as he drove. After a few moments of electrical silence he laughed and gently removed her hand.

"We'll never get to Marblehead," he chided, "if you don't go slow."

"What would have happened," Penny wondered out loud, "if you hadn't come down to the galley and found me alone?"

"Something else," he replied confidently.

Penny smiled. "You seem so sure."

"I am." He reached over and caressed her cheek with the back of his hand. "The thing about me is even though I'm sometimes terribly dense, eventually information does penetrate."

"How do you mean?" Penny hung eagerly on his every word.

"That morning you ran into me as I was getting out of the swimming pool . . . and you apologized to me?"

"Yes," Penny said.

"I just couldn't admit to myself that you really meant it. I kept telling myself you were a phony, a game player like everyone else. It wasn't that I considered Pierre some stiff competition or anything. I just told myself you were playing those old 'I'll make him jealous now' kind of games."

"I didn't . . . intentionally," Penny replied.

"I know that." Joel threw her a warm smile. "I knew it then, only my pride wouldn't let me admit it."

Penny shook her head. "It's important to nip those kind of misunderstandings in the bud."

Joel nodded solemnly. "You didn't have any supper. Are you hungry?"

"What I want tonight is not food," said Penny softly, and they drove the remaining minutes in silence.

When they finally pulled into the parking lot outside the New England Yacht Club it was nearly two in the morning, but Penny was as vibrant and energized as if she had had a good night's sleep.

"Almost home." Joel slipped his arm around her waist and they walked through the dewy grass toward their rooms.

Home, thought Penny, and her heart leaped at what suddenly seemed a very real possibility. What would it be like to share her life with this dynamic man? Home. The word seemed to encompass them both, and something in the way Joel had intoned it gave her the distinct impression that for him it was a wish.

"I have a bottle of champagne," he observed. "The same bottle you declined . . . how many nights ago?"

"Only a week." Penny smiled happily, and suddenly she had the wild urge to tell him she loved him. The words wanted release; they raged inside of her along with her desire for him.

". . . and some canned pâté that isn't too bad." Joel fished in the pocket of his jacket for his keys, then stopped suddenly as he noticed that a light was burning in his room.

"Who the hell could that be?" he muttered, and Penny experienced a chill of apprehension.

Joel's door was ajar. He opened it slowly, warily, then rushed in when he saw Max, who was sitting on the edge of Joel's bed practically enveloped in cigarette smoke.

"You took long enough!" Max jumped to his feet and cast a brief, angry glance at Penny before continuing in a frantic voice.

"Tippy wants to talk to you," Max said.

"It's almost two thirty." Joel's face fell.

Max shook his head and ran his hand nervously through his

thinning hair. "It's urgent. You've got to go talk to her. Believe me . . . she . . ."

"All right," Joel said tightly.

Penny blinked unbelievingly. Could the same event be repeating itself? Why did both of these men jump every time Tippy crooked her little finger?

"Is she sick?" Penny could not hide her disappointment.

Max shook his head emphatically. "No, she's not sick!"

"Then . . ." Penny broke off and looked imploringly at Joel.

"Let's hurry," Max tugged urgently at Joel's arm.

"I'll explain later." Joel moved to Penny's side as Max practically ran out of the room.

"Joel . . . come on!" Max stuck his head inside the door.

"Get some sleep." Joel brushed his lips against Penny's in a perfunctory kiss which felt more like a bucket of cold water.

In a daze Penny turned off the lights in his room and let herself into her own room. She felt abandoned and utterly at a loss. Was it possible that mere moments before she had been on the brink of blurting out to this man how much she loved him?

She paced restlessly around the room feeling deprived. Her senses were heightened, she was on the brink, and here she was pacing around like a cat in heat. No, it was more than that. *Everything* had been interrupted. Couldn't he have at least taken the time to explain? Or perhaps it wasn't important to him that she not be worried or upset. It seemed that the minute Tippy's name came up he was unable to focus on anything else.

No, she argued with herself, he said he would explain later. She must not jump to any conclusions simply because she was disappointed.

But she was too keyed up to sleep and she kept looking at the clock and wondering when he would be coming back to his room. The marvelous sensual peace that had filled her for the past hours was supplanted by a wary edginess.

She picked up the volume of Edgar Allan Poe and tried to read, but the words blurred before her eyes, so she tossed the book aside and moved outside to the terrace. Never had she felt her aloneness in such an acutely negative way. The moon, lower on the horizon now, was the same moon that had seemed to smile down on her when they were still on board the *Luscious.* Now it seemed to taunt her and she resented it just as she resented Joel for having so much power over her emotions.

Her body ached and throbbed with the memory of his searing strength pulsating inside her. They should be together now! If it had not been for some neurotic demand on Tippy's part they would have, by this time, drunk their champagne and been luxuriating in each other. She would have fallen asleep nestled against his warm, yielding body, and tomorrow morning she would have wakened to the exciting sensation of those long tapering fingers that seemed to possess the most intimate knowledge of her needs and desires.

She moved back inside her room and, shucking the caftan in the dark, slipped naked beneath the cool white sheets. But sleep would not come nor could she content herself with pleasant memories of the shattering experience in the cabin on board the *Luscious.* As her frustration mounted so did her panic, and as the numbers on the small digital clock clicked off the passage of the night, her imagination seemed hell-bent on torturing her.

Flushed with night's panic, she leaped out of bed and wriggled into her old swimming suit. Perhaps she could work off some of her frustration by swimming a few laps in the pool. She shivered as she dropped the large beach towel to the ground, and as she stood poised on the edge of the pool she tried not to glance off to the right to see if there was a light still burning in Tippy's room.

After ten brisk laps she pulled herself breathlessly out of the pool, toweled down quickly, and still breathing heavily from the exertion, ran back to her room. She paused outside Joel's room. A light was burning. Hadn't she turned off the lights? She raised her hand to knock at his door, thought better of it, and went back inside her own room.

Perhaps he had called? Yes, what if he had phoned and not finding her in was sitting up worrying about her?

Penny stood indecisively in the middle of the room, unaware that her lips were chattering and that a pool of water had begun to form at her feet. She stiffened at the muffled sound of Joel's voice, and her heart seemed to stop as she recognized the faint timbre of Tippy's reply.

Of course she couldn't hear through the wall, and she was mortified that she would even strain so to try. What on earth was she doing?

She tore off her wet swimming suit and stomped into the bathroom. Again she had the uncanny sensation that she was not herself, that some raging, jealous spirit had taken possession of her soul . . . and her sanity. As she stepped under the steaming shower, hot tears streamed down her cheeks . . . tears of disappointment in herself.

Well, of course! She had been a fool. It was always a mistake not to trust one's first instinct, and her first instinct had been not to trust Joel Sanborne. She had never, *ever* wanted to become involved with an actor, and unlike most of the young women at the studio had never been enamored of the more glamorous aspects of the profession. With Joel . . . with any actor for that matter, there would always be something. If it wasn't a tearful costar it would be a fan or lengthy out-of-town obligations, that would mean long separations unless she became simply a follower.

Which, she told herself adamantly as she stepped out of the shower, she had no intention of becoming. Now, thoughts of their earlier passion were almost totally obliterated by her rising fury at Joel. She was tempted to knock on his door, to interrupt his little tryst with Tippy, to. . . .

A shrill ring of the phone interrupted her mental tirade. She stomped over to answer it with her chin thrust forward.

"Will you ever forgive me?" Joel's deep baritone was filled with repentance. Penny felt her mind slip into a catatonic state. She had wrapped a towel around her waist and her breasts hung free. Dimly she was aware that her nipples had hardened into expectant pleasure points at the sound of his voice.

"Penny? . . . Penny, are you there?"

"Yes," her voice but not her mind replied to his inquiry.

"Did I wake you?" Joel questioned with an apologetic note in his voice.

Suddenly a sense of relief flowed through her body, and her humor, along with her voice, returned. She laughed softly.

"What does that mean?" Joel said after a moment.

"It means I'm not asleep. I haven't been asleep." Penny sank onto her rumpled bed.

"Do you want a visitor?" Joel's voice took on a hushed, seductive tone, and Penny's heart began to race.

"It's three thirty," she whispered.

"Good," came his reply. "I can make love to you for another three hours before it's light."

"And then what?" Penny fell languidly back on her bed.

"I turn into . . ." He gave a wicked laugh. "Why not find out what I turn into."

Penny closed her eyes, savoring the delicious sensations that the sound of his voice evoked in her. She waited for him to continue, and it was several seconds before she realized that he had hung up the phone. By the time she did realize it, there was a knock at her door.

She ran to the door and threw it open, totally unaware that she was naked from the waist up. Joel's mouth flew open at the sight of her tight, erect breasts, and instantly her hands flew across to cover them.

Without a word Joel closed the door behind him, then with one hand he moved her hands aside and caressed her breasts with loving eyes. Dreamily he moved his gaze back to her face, and as he did he reached for one breast, tracing his middle finger lightly around the perimeter of its rosy nipple. He glanced back at her to observe her response, and the look in his eye stirred something deep within her. He held her eye as he traced an erotic pattern around the stiff nipple.

Penny stood absolutely still as his other hand moved to the top of the towel, which was wrapped loosely around her waist. He removed it easily, and his eyes left hers to travel slowly down the length of her willowy form until she knew by the expression on his face that they had come to rest on that source that was now throbbing urgently for him. He smiled softly, and with a smooth glance at her rapt expression placed his hand very tenderly on the source of his fascination.

"So soft," he crooned with downcast eyes as one finger slipped inside to titillate. Penny reached out to him, and he took her hand as he sank to his knees in front of her. She moaned, swaying above him and grasping his dark hair in her hands as she called out his name in a voice thick with desire.

All were such new sensations for her. Vaguely she was aware that with him she was totally uninhibited, as if he had unleashed a new Penny who had been hiding submissively for all these years. She thrust herself toward him to give him greater access to those moist recesses he coveted. Yes, with Joel Sanborne she was a new woman. And what did that mean?

She smiled lazily and steadied herself when a new current of pleasure rippled through her. Her boldness with him astonished her, but then everything he did was done so naturally. He did not need to *be* sexy; he was in his every gesture the most thrillingly erotic creature she had ever encountered. It was this powerful animal magnetism his fans responded to. Yet she really doubted if anyone would guess that together with the magnetism, the vitality, and the erotic playfulness he was fully the most sensitive and considerate lover one could imagine.

"Oh, Joel, I want you now," Penny whispered, and unable to tolerate the glow he had created, she took his hand and pulled him back up to his feet. As he rose his eyes were black with wanting. She felt proud, and when he moved her hand to his belt she proceeded swiftly to unfasten the little silver buckle.

She gave him a wanton smile as she tugged at his trousers, and in a matter of moments they stood trembling in each other's presence. Their earlier forays on the *Luscious* had been performed in almost Stygian darkness, and now in the soft light of

Penny's room they reveled in the full sensual luster of each other's bodies.

"God, you're beautiful." Joel took one step toward her and ran his hand along her silken flank. His hand persuaded her to turn around and a moment later Penny felt him pressing against her rounded behind. Fervently she wheeled around and pressed into him, but he was in no rush and once again he turned her away, his eyes caressing her, driving her closer and closer to the edge.

His eyes alone seemed to have the power to ignite her fully. He took one breast playfully in his mouth and teased it as he eased her down onto the bed, and when she fell breathlessly back on her pillow he showered kisses on her tender inner thigh.

She was at such a pitch of excitement that she put her knuckle against her mouth to keep from screaming. But this was only the beginning. Joel moved his mouth across her ivory abdomen, enticing her further, and finally releasing her from the edge of pain, he pressed the full force of his steely body into her soft pliant curves.

"You're so beautiful," he murmured again as he locked his strong arms under her. "We have nothing to do but enjoy ourselves. No phone . . ." He reached out and lifted the receiver off the hook. "We have all day tomorrow and all night tomorrow. We are incommunicado to the world. Is that all right with you?"

Penny murmured her approval as her hands explored the muscles of his hips. She marveled at the differences between them and closed her eyes to savor each lovely detail.

"Did that mean yes?" Joel raised up slightly to peer into her love-glazed eyes.

"Mmmm." Penny smiled languidly, then as his hand sought out that supreme point of pleasure, she cried out. He stroked her until she arched toward him, then feeling the power of his manliness coiled for striking, she dug her fingers deeper into his back. She was in a near fever of exquisite agony, wanting once again to feel the fury of his might filling her. She reached for him but he held her hand back.

"I take it the idea appeals to you?" He was panting with desire, but his dark eyes laughed as he looked down at her.

"Oh, Joel, don't tease me now!" Penny cried, so near exploding that she began moving involuntarily.

"My love!" Joel's large hands seemed to devour her body as he surged inside of her.

"I love you," Penny whispered hoarsely as they moved in one rhythm. The words seemed to thunder throughout her entire body as if they were a part of the cataclysmic motion. There was no way to separate those words from the myriad ecstasies that shook her.

"My God . . . how I love you." As dawn crept into the room Joel raised himself above her and smoothed her damp, passion-fevered brow with his hand.

## CHAPTER EIGHT

He loved her! He had said it. She had said it over and over again. "I love you, Joel." The world had taken on a kaleidoscope of new colors. Her serious green eyes held an intense new light, and there was absolutely nothing that she could not accomplish. This new energy coursing through her body gave her an almost invincible sense of her own power, and as she lay next to Joel's sleeping body she wondered if it would ever be possible for her to fall asleep again. Plans jumped into her mind . . . all sorts of plans from reupholstering her ratty sofa in New York to raising several million dollars to make her own film starring Joel Sanborne. As the lazy Sunday world outside her room came to life she planned to cut her hair, grow her nails, recaulk the bathroom tiles, enroll in a French class, learn how to play racketball, write postcards to her parents and her sisters, and buy Joel a volume of Anne Sexton's poetry—all at the first available opportunity.

She could not sleep! She glanced at him and saw that he was sleeping soundly with a lopsided, contented smile on his lips. It was already eleven o'clock, but they hadn't fallen asleep (rather, Joel hadn't) until eight. She stretched deliciously underneath the sheet and her body felt voluptuous and utterly at peace. Only her mind danced with ideas, plots, plans.

As soon as she got back to New York she would begin doing some serious research to try and find a project that she and Joel could do together. The more she thought about him as an actor, the more excited she was at the prospect of seeing him sink his teeth into a really good part. It would be such a challenge to work with him. Well, she wasn't kidding herself that it would be easy. No doubt there would be problems . . . even if they could raise the necessary money. She guessed that Joel would balk at the idea. But she was ready for him. If years as a daytime television villain had soured him and turned him a trifle cynical, she would combat his negativity with her own incredible optimism. The more she thought about it the more stimulated she became, and when the digital clock indicated that it was noon she finally admitted to herself that there was not the remotest chance that she would fall asleep. She stared at Joel intently, willing him to wake up, and when he continued to sleep peacefully she resorted to making little noises in her throat . . . just in case he really wasn't *that* deeply asleep.

Finally she slid quietly out of bed, brushed her teeth, combed her hair, and put on her bathing suit. She tiptoed out of the room and went outside to sit by the pool. She waved at Faye and several of the other crew but chose to remain in a quieter area where she sank into one of the chaise longues and immediately fell asleep.

Somehow her slumber was made all the more delicious by the noisy, fun-filled racket in the nearby swimming pool. Several times she shifted on the narrow chaise, raising her languid body up to look groggily around. As long, late-afternoon shadows fell across the rippling blue waters and the gusty echoes of swimmers dimmed, she opened her eyes. Joel, dressed casually in white trousers and a red and white T-shirt which strained across the smooth muscles of his chest, was smiling down at her.

"Hi," she said, squinting drowsily.

"Hi yourself." He knelt down next to her and planted a light kiss on her slightly sunburned nose.

"What time is it?" Penny stretched her long, bronzed legs and pulled herself up to a sitting position as Joel thrust his wristwatch in front of her face. She blinked, focused, and looked up into his grinning face.

"Time for dinner." He patted her on the back, then drew her to her feet and led her back to her room, directing her to shower and dress and join him in the terrace dining room as soon as she was presentable.

"What a peculiar day." Penny smiled radiantly as she joined him at a secluded table. Her sandy hair was smooth and shiny as it fell in its smart cut around her glowing, tanned face. Joel's eyes drank in her fresh, unadorned beauty—the smart white linen suit which she wore with a plain peach-colored tank top, her white straw Italian shoes with the tiny heels, one slender gold bracelet, and a pair of delicate gold drop earrings.

"Did anyone ever tell you, Miss Penelope Phillips, that you are a knockout?" He stood and helped her into her chair.

"Not exactly." Penny blushed with pride at his compliment. The truth was she felt positively ravishing.

Joel stared across the table at her as though he were mesmerized. He looked around the sparsely-peopled terrace furtively, then returned his dark, impetuous eyes to her.

"A light but sumptuous dinner and then early to bed. How does that sound to you?" His voice was low and heavy with promises.

"It sounds perfect," Penny replied, reveling in the heady implications of his suggestive manner.

"However"—she tore her eyes away from his—"Max phoned while I was in the shower. He was slightly evasive but clearly upset."

"What about?" Joel interjected with an uneasy shift of his large frame.

Penny stifled a flicker of annoyance. That concern, she suspected, had something to do with Tippy. But she didn't want to think about Tippy now. She had considered questioning him about last night but rejected the idea. She wanted nothing to mar the absolute perfection of the day.

110

"Business," she answered. "The show. He's afraid we haven't covered ourselves with the scenes we shot on Thursday and Friday. He's toying with the idea of sending me back to New York so I can take a look at them."

Joel frowned and looked perplexed. He gave the waiter their drink order, then looked back at Penny.

"I don't think he will. I just think he's generally nervous about the shoot. Anyhow, he wants me to have breakfast with him at six tomorrow morning."

Joel nodded tightly, and when the waiter returned with Penny's white wine and Joel's scotch, he sipped it pensively.

"What is it?" Penny asked after a moment.

"Nothing." Joel shook his head.

"That"—Penny met his brooding eyes directly—"was very unconvincing."

"You read me pretty well," Joel remarked wryly.

"What's on your mind?" Penny persisted.

"Disappointment." He smiled ruefully, and Penny's heart seemed about to burst with joy that he could feel such acute emotion at the idea of being separated from her. She reached across the table and took his large hand in her two slender ones.

"We can be together tonight," she whispered. "And if I have to fly back to New York, which I seriously doubt I will, it will only be for one day. I'll fly back the same night."

Joel gave her a feeble smile, and she sensed that something else was bothering him deeply, that his reaction was not simply to the possibility that she might disappear for a length of time. She made one more attempt to coax him into telling her what was really on his mind, but he evaded her by launching into his favorite topic, France. Penny saw that he was able to submerge whatever was on his mind. Remarkably, he turned on the San-borne charm and entertained her with anecdote after anecdote about his various trips abroad.

He ordered a fine white Burgundy, a Meursault of an excellent vintage, and as they sipped its dry, fruity essence he elaborated on the beauties of the ancient province of Burgundy. By the time

111

their delicately sautéed gray sole arrived, they were flushed and appropriately loquacious from the wine.

As they were completing the fish and beginning on their salads, Max and Tippy stepped onto the terrace and took a table deep in the shadows. Penny was about to point out their presence to Joel when a glance at his face stopped her. His brow was knit, his dark eyes filled with something she had never seen there. What was it?

Somewhat shaken, she returned her attention to her salad. Pain, that was what she had seen in his eyes. Something more than worry, something stronger than deep concern.

"I'd better not," Penny declined when Joel suggested they have coffee and brandy.

"You're right." He smiled. "So good to have a sensible companion."

Penny's eyes searched his face for a trace of the apprehension she had read there earlier, but it was gone. He seemed to her suddenly too foreign, too complex and changeable. For an instant she felt a rush of panic at the idea of loving a man who seemed quite capable of assuming various colors at a moment. Yes, sometimes, as he had said earlier, she could read him. But at other times his dark eyes were fathomless, his smile . . . perhaps nothing more than those full, sensuous lips she loved widening across his even white teeth.

As they left the terrace she was aware that he skirted around the opposite direction so that they would not have to pass by Tippy and Max. Again she resisted the temptation to question him, and by the time they had walked across the lush verdant lawn and were standing nose to nose outside her door, the scent of him, the warmth exuding from his powerful body, had dimmed all of her questions.

She handed him the key to her room, and wordlessly he opened the door and led her inside.

The next morning when the digital buzzed, Penny's eyes flew open and her heart raced with alarm. He was gone! She leaped

112

out of bed and only then did she see one of her yellow legal pads propped up against the lamp that was next to the digital clock.

She read his note voraciously and fell back on the bed feeling the tension drain from her body. He had wakened during the night and, unable to fall back asleep and not wanting to disturb her, had returned to his own room. He would see her at work and would she please keep this evening open for a drive to nearby Concord where he knew a wonderful little inn. The note was signed *love, Joel,* and he had done an amusing sketch of a bleary-eyed man next to his signature.

After a quick shower Penny dressed in jeans and an oversize T-shirt imprinted with the *Dream of Life* logo. She left her room at a gallop, and at six on the dot was seated at a table in the small breakfast room in the main house. While she waited for Max she sipped the rich black coffee and read through the day's script. They had fallen asleep early, and she had had a deep and nourishing sleep. She felt fabulous, looking forward to a day's work and later the evening with Joel. Wasn't that an absolutely ideal combination?

Max was late. She considered phoning his room but thought better of it. She stared out the window at the dewy lawn which was dotted with plump robins foraging for an early, wormy breakfast.

"Sorry." Around seven Max slid into the chair across from her and waved to the waitress for an immediate cup of coffee.

"Bad night?" Penny was alarmed at the gray pallor of his complexion.

"No worse than usual," Max answered with a distracted smile. "I see you were taking advantage of my tardiness to get some work done." He nodded curtly at the pile of scripts next to Penny's empty coffee cup.

"I'd done them before," she said, defending his oblique criticism with a smile. "If I'm not mistaken we have a comparatively easy day ahead of us."

"Mmmm." Max smacked his lips noncommittaly as he took his first sip of coffee. "You order?"

113

Penny shook her head. "I just feel like coffee. I always indulge in those pastries they bring to the location. Even when they're soggy, I can't seem to resist them."

"I'll have the melon and a double order of cinnamon toast," Max told the waitress.

"This isn't easy," Max said, turning back to Penny after the waitress had disappeared.

Penny's stomach tightened. She stared at Max incredulously as if he had already fired her.

"I know you think you want to be a director"—he avoided looking directly at her and she was thankful—"but . . . I just have the feeling you're not ready for it. You're not very realistic."

He paused and Penny waited for him to continue, her hands gripping the sides of the chair.

"You should have told me about that incident with Archie," he accused directly.

"I . . . I didn't want to bother you," Penny stammered defensively.

"What did you plan to do about it?" Max interrogated.

"I did what I could. I went ahead and shot some long shots with Irene. I tried to take advantage of the time."

"Of course," Max said tightly, "but we both know you were just marking time . . . treading water. You simply did not deal with the real issue."

Penny lowered her eyes, stung by Max's harsh perception of how she had handled herself. She fought not to reply bitterly that it seemed totally unjust, that the repercussions from Archie's unprofessional behavior were coming down hard on her head.

The waitress brought Max's melon, and he attacked it ferociously. What was behind this lecture, Penny wondered. It wasn't like Max to talk to her in this manner.

"You do want to direct?" He questioned again, and she nodded. "Well, then don't you see that talent, whatever talent you might have, is the least of your problems? If you can't keep the actors in front of the camera you don't have much of a chance, do you? We will never get to see all that talent, will we?"

114

"I couldn't believe he was leaving," Penny said numbly.

"That's what I mean." Max looked at her narrowly. "You weren't facing reality. Your eyes told you he was leaving, but you didn't do anything about it. Look, if you're really serious about this, Penny, you've got to be more aggressive."

"Did Archie come to you and complain?" Penny felt a surge of anger.

"That's neither here nor there. *You* should have been able to keep control of the situation. Archie's not a difficult fellow. My God, if you have problems with Arch, what the hell are you going to do when faced with a temperamental actor or actress? What are you going to do when someone starts yelling at you or throwing a tantrum?"

"I understand." Penny took a deep breath and looked directly at Max. "And you're right," she admitted tightly. "I opted for the easy out."

She started to get up, but Max caught her by the hand. "You know I like you . . ."

"I guess you do," Penny said flatly.

"See you out at the mansion in half an hour," Max called as she walked dejectedly out of the little breakfast room.

Well, she thought, that was that. Her chances of returning to New York with any meaningful film were nil. Max would never entrust her with any important scenes after that. Damn Archie!

The adrenaline coursed through her body as she trudged along the road that led to the mansion. Archie was a pain, but blaming him would accomplish nothing. As long as she made him the problem, the problem would continue to exist *in her.*

It did not take a professional psychiatrist to understand why Archie had decided to react the way he had. He was paying her back. It was as simple as that. He had made two attempts to escalate their relationship to something more intimate, and she had rejected him. He had walked off the set not because she was a woman or an amateur, as he had called her, but because she had rejected him. And he probably knew she had been seeing Joel, which irked him further.

As she climbed the steps to the mansion she spotted him standing under a leafy maple, smoking a cigarette. She approached him tentatively with no idea what she would say. They had not spoken directly since he had walked off the set.

"Nice morning," she began.

"Going to be hot." Archie looked at her warily.

"Archie, you and I have never had any problems before, and I'd like to call a halt to this . . . feud before it goes any further."

"Look," he said to her, "I did what I had to do. I left because I'm the guy whose face appears on the screen. It all comes back to me and I didn't . . . don't think you have the experience."

"I think you wanted to humiliate me, embarrass me," Penny said staunchly.

"Why would I?" Archie pretended to be shocked.

Penny paused. She knew perfectly well why he would want to and so did he. But saying so, naming the reason, would only alienate him further. She searched for some tact, something midway between the complete truth and a bold-faced lie that might let him off the hook and at the same time let him know that she would not be dallied with.

"I don't know why," she lied, "but you did humiliate me and just when I needed someone like you to help. Look, I'm not in competition with you. You know I respect your work as an actor. If I gave you some direction you couldn't tolerate you certainly know me well enough to know that I am a reasonable person. I would have listened to your objections, and we would have come to an agreement. I could have learned something from you, Archie."

Archie studied his blue jogging shoe intently, and Penny sensed that her words had softened him. By not accusing him, perhaps she had begun to gain his respect.

"I'm very serious about my work," she said slowly. "I have every intention of becoming a good, recognized director."

Archie looked at her briefly. Her implication was clear and her manner of stating it persuasive: directors hired actors. It was not unlikely that sometime in the future she could be holding the reins. One day it was just possible that Archer Marshall might need something from Penelope Phillips.

"Let's be friends, all right?" Penny extended her hand, and after a moment Archie took it in a firm clasp.

The day's filming proceeded smoothly until late afternoon when light showers forced them to call it a day. Joel was immediately at Penny's side to whisk her into his Porsche and drive her back to the Yacht Club to change. Rain or not, he intended to drive to Concord so that they could pay homage to various Revolutionary War sites as well as to those nineteenth-century American philosophers Emerson and Thoreau.

"Besides," he said when she returned to the car dressed in a soft beige silk dress covered by her serviceable khaki trench coat, "the sun is bound to come out again by five."

As they wound their way out of the enigmatic, twisting Marblehead streets, the rain drove so hard against the windshield that Penny urged him to turn around. But no . . . he was determined, and sure enough, by the time they pulled onto Route 95 South the rain had stopped, and by the time they arrived in the historic village of Concord, the world was bathed in a glistening, majestic light.

Joel dug a dog-eared guidebook out of his glove compartment, and together they wandered around Concord, their feet soaked from puddles, their spirits high.

For dinner Joel had made a reservation at a nearby inn that was reputed to be the oldest in the United States. The Longfellow Wayside Inn was a charming spot, and perhaps because of the erratic weather, it was practically deserted. Since the drive back to Marblehead was short, Joel and Penny decided they could afford to linger over one more coffee and a touch of brandy.

"I like the way you dress." Joel leaned back in his chair to view her. "Simple and elegant . . . none of that trendy stuff. I am so tired of fashionplates," he said with a grimace.

Penny laughed. "I'm afraid I don't have the nerve to wear any of the more adventurous styles. Can you imagine me in one of

117

those short ruffled mini-dresses with little white bobby sox and my hair dyed green in a punk cut?"

Joel laughed. "No. Thank God!" He studied her a moment and smacked his lips appreciatively. "It's good to get away from the group."

Penny giggled. "I'd say we were pretty far away from the group all day yesterday."

"I mean geographically away. Sometimes," he observed, "just leaving a place can give you a new perspective. That's why I insist on having a car in New York. I can't tell you the number of times I just hop behind the wheel and drive maybe forty-five minutes outside the city and stop at some diner for a hamburger."

Penny nodded and after a moment she found herself telling him both about Max's unjust response to Archie's walking off the set and her later confrontation with Archie.

"The thing I'm pleased about," she concluded, "is that I was able to talk to Archie without feeling that I had prove that I was right and he was wrong . . . even though he was wrong. I was able to look ahead and determine what would benefit me the most in the long run. And in the long run . . . I need Archie's cooperation. I need that more than I need him to know that I think he's a bit of a swine, a hypocrite, etc., etc."

A flicker of concern colored Joel's face. "You're really serious about this directing, aren't you?"

"Of course I am." Penny refused to acknowledge the edge that had come into his voice.

"And on a sliding scale from one to ten how would you rate your . . . your ambitiousness?" he asked.

"Don't be silly," she said, laughing. "You can't rate ambition."

"Just for the fun of it," said Joel, but somehow Penny did not think he saw any fun in it. He seemed almost defensive.

"Let's say," she began carefully, "that I intend to do everything within my power to achieve the professional stature I think

I deserve. I know that luck enters into it, but to a large extent I believe that people make their own luck."

"And I take it your job as Max's assistant is just a step on the ladder to success."

"It's hard for a woman," she said intensely. She desperately wanted him to understand.

"I know it is," he acquiesced with a brief smile before his face clouded over once again. "The few woman directors I know have sacrificed a great deal."

Penny bristled. "Anyone who enters a tough profession like this suffers a great deal. Not just women. Look at you—look how that fan manhandled you the other day. Look at Max. I'd say Max was suffering a great deal on this remote. In a way, my temperament is better suited to this sort of pressure than is Max's."

Joel eyed her narrowly, but she continued. "Max has always been terribly excitable, and he's been even more so since we came to Massachusetts."

"And you're not the excitable type?" Joel queried with a touch of cynicism that made her pause.

She frowned, thinking of the panic she had fallen into the night before last when he had gone to see Tippy. Could she honestly say she wasn't the excitable type after that?

She twisted her mouth and nibbled her upper lip thoughtfully. She had always perceived herself to be infinitely responsible, rational . . . sometimes to the point of being cool. Compared to most people she observed, she was very calm. Only since her involvement with Joel had she grown erratic and unpredictable.

"Well . . . ?" He was waiting for her reply with a sullen expression.

"Yes," she uttered reluctantly. "Yes, I am less excitable than most people. I work well under pressure and I rarely lose my temper. I know I have a lot to learn about working with actors and about the camera itself, but I really want to learn, and isn't that half the battle?"

"I suppose so." Joel reached for the check with a desultory smile.

All during the drive back to Marblehead Joel seemed moody, as if her enthusiasm for her future as a director had depressed him. In the uneasy silence she wracked her brain to think of something to say, but all areas of conversation seemed to have dried up. Even her effort to begin conversation on France did not elicit any response. Finally she resorted to telling him about her long search for a new apartment, a story that bored even her but at least it filled the silence. He feigned an interest she knew he did not have, and together they carried on a superficial discussion about New York real estate and the dearth of decent housing. Their words were hollow, and even their voices, thought Penny, had an empty ring.

As they walked across the damp, spongy lawn back at the Yacht Club, Penny slipped her arm through his. He squeezed it, and for an instant she thought that whatever rift had come between them might magically dissolve. If he would take her in his arms the world would once again be right.

She glanced at his stony profile, longing to brush her lips against those high, Indian-like cheekbones and soften the rigidity that had come over him.

"Can I come in?" He did not look at her, and there was an all-too-proper tone to his inquiry.

Penny nodded dumbly and switched on the light as they entered her room.

"I should tell you something." He stood hesitantly just inside the door. Penny's throat constricted as she waited for him to continue.

"These past few days," he began, "have meant a great deal to me."

Penny's green eyes were filled with apprehension as she waited. His words indicated a favorable response to her and their time spent together, but his manner was downright despondent.

"Joel, maybe we should talk some other time . . . maybe we're both tired and . . ." Penny broke off with a confused gesture. She had no idea why she did not want to hear what he had to say, but somehow she felt strongly that this was the wrong time for a serious discussion.

Joel glanced at her sharply. "I thought you liked the direct, honest approach."

Penny shrugged and sat across the room from him. The digital clock indicated that it was nearly ten o'clock. The last thing in the world she wanted was an argument before she went to bed. They both needed a good night's sleep, for the next few days would be long and arduous. He must have seen her glancing at the clock, for he approached her with a surly, argumentative stance.

"Worried about the time?" His tone was smug. He knew he had read her mind.

"I can see"—she placed her hands together calmly—"that you have something rather serious on your mind, and I think it would be foolish to get into it tonight."

"I guess I'm witnessing the famous Phillips control," he said snidely. "Don't you ever get emotional?"

Penny pressed her lips together and looked away from him. If only he knew how dissolved and helpless she had felt the other night. If only he knew how her heart was aching and pounding with distress even as he glowered down at her.

"I have to be up again at five thirty," she answered and was shocked at the sharp tone that had come into her voice.

"So that's it." He laughed rudely. "It doesn't matter what I have to say. Business always comes first!"

"Joel . . . please!" Penny sprang to her feet and put her hands beseechingly on his chest. "Can't you see you're trying to start a fight and—"

"And you don't want to fight?" He made no move to turn away from her, and she could feel the life throbbing in his body.

*This is ridiculous,* she thought as her arms went around his neck and her body molded itself against his hard angular form. She felt him shiver at the recognition of her soft, pliant curves. His mouth opened against hers, and his large hands spread

121

fanlike against her hips as she pressed her body against his rising passion.

"What are you doing?" He pulled away from her, his face flushed from the conflict of desire and anger.

"I want to settle"—she tried to smile—"out of court. Please, let's not argue! I don't even know what we're arguing about."

"Because," he shouted, "you won't listen! You want everything nice and smooth. Well, the world isn't a nice smooth place. Max was right when he said you were unrealistic. I listen to you talk about your professional future, and it's like listening to a starry-eyed adolescent."

Penny shrank from his anger. What right had he to accuse her? What fury of his own was driving him to take it out on her?

"Listen, I've come to a few conclusions over the past week. I had wanted to share them with you until you let me know that it was far more important for you to get your sleep." Joel started angrily for the door.

"Go ahead," Penny blurted out. "You've already ruined whatever *calm* I'd managed to retain!"

Joel paused with his hand on the doorknob, then crossed back to her. "I've decided I'm tired of being clawed by fans, tired of memorizing script after script of mediocre, sappy material. I want to do something meaningful in my life!"

There was a passionate urgency in his voice as he spoke, and despite her anger and confusion Penny felt awed both by the vehemence of his passion and by his power.

"I need to know that my life has value . . . that I'm not simply some toy . . . a voice and an image to be turned on and off at whim. I've decided to quit the show. I'm going to go back to law school . . . move away from the city, far away to some place human like Minnesota or . . . or New Mexico." Joel broke off. He seemed to be waiting for her to respond, but she could only stare miserably at the thin Oriental carpet on the floor of her room. She felt dizzy, too confused to make any effort at communication.

"Why are you telling me this now?" she asked after a long silence. "We were having a wonderful time . . . why did you—"

"Because," Joel interrupted her abruptly, "it's clear that you and I are traveling along different paths. It's pretty obvious that there's no future for us!"

His voice rose in intensity, and Penny watched as he moved brusquely to the door. When he was gone she sat with her hands clutched in her lap. She stared at her knuckles, which were white in contrast to her tanned fingers. She wanted to cry but she could not. She heard him close the door to his room and wondered whether he too wasn't sitting in just such a desolate position. No future for them? His reasoning confounded her, but she hadn't the least doubt that he had meant what he'd said.

# CHAPTER NINE

"I'll have the seafood crêpe," Irene bubbled, "and a glass of tomato juice."

Penny continued to stare forlornly at the menu. The words seemed scrambled and meaningless. The idea of food was odious. "A cup of the soup du jour," she told the waitress finally.

"And to drink?" The waitress's smile intruded on her misery, and she blinked as if someone had just awakened her. "Hot tea," she replied.

Penny looked grimly around the little Victorian tea room where she and Irene were having lunch. An entire day had passed since Joel had announced that there was no future for them. He had done his best in the interim to prove his point.

"Talk to him," Irene urged. "Penny, you can't walk around feeling like a zombie for the rest of your life."

"The rest of my life?" Penny flinched. "Irene, don't exaggerate. I'll get over it."

"Maybe not." Irene viewed her friend's unhappy face with sympathy.

"Will you stop being the voice of doom?" Penny tried to laugh. Irene had become very tanned over the past week and a half, and the contrast between her fair hair, blue eyes, and dark skin made her even more beautiful than usual. Penny felt a pang of envy, not only for Irene's blossoming beauty, but for Irene's happiness with Pierre, which seemed to be enduring and growing. Pierre doted on Irene, and Penny had never seen the younger woman more relaxed and confident.

"Why don't you two talk it over?" Irene persisted. "Just tell him you'll move wherever he wants to live. You said he was talking about leaving New York City. So just tell him that's fine with you."

"But it isn't fine with me." Penny smiled at Irene's naïve solution.

"Pierre's talking about moving back to France," Irene elaborated. "I said . . . fine. When are we leaving?"

"You could really just abandon your acting career like that?" Penny was intrigued by the differences in their attitudes.

"Sure," Irene said, then smiled as the waitress set the steaming crêpes down in front of her.

"I envy you," Penny declared, staring at her cup of soup. "Anyway, I'm just not sure if that's really the issue between Joel and me."

"Then you should find out what is the issue." Irene was savoring her crêpes with a dreamy expression. "You're in love with him, you dope—you can't just let things go."

Penny smiled wanly at Irene's accurate if simplistic interpretation of things. But it was true; she couldn't just let things go. And the longer she waited the more difficult the confrontation was going to be. Already she and Joel were hardening in their positions. Only maybe she had misread him. Perhaps he had contrived his untimely outburst as a way of breaking off with her before her feelings became even more involved. Only her feelings were already too involved, and surely he had known that. And what about his words? *I love you.* Hadn't he meant them?

Maybe not. Penny tried not to gag on the clam chowder. Maybe he had just been carried away by the passion of the moment. It wouldn't be the first time that someone uttered those none-too-sacred words without meaning them. Or perhaps he had meant them at the time and only later discovered that he had been acting the part of devoted lover.

She was exhausted from trying to figure it all out. At Irene's suggestion they went into the little Victorian boutique that was located next to the tea room. Penny thought nostalgically of that first conversation she had had with Joel while looking in the display window at the delicate items.

"Oh look, Pen!" Irene picked out a white petticoat with eyelet and lace panels down the front. "You should wear something like this."

Penny shook her head gloomily, and her mind went back to her last evening with Joel when he had complimented her on her clothes. Why had he done that? Why compliment her and treat her so warmly when all that evening he must have known he had no interest in continuing with her.

Penny moved away from Irene and closed her eyes against the tears that threatened to overflow. This wasn't like her. . . . Crying in private was a rare enough experience, but crying in public? But suddenly she could not put the image of Joel's dark eyes out of her mind. It seemed she could almost feel the weight of him on her naked body, and the image of those luminous eyes as his face was lowered above hers made her catch her breath. The impact of what it would mean to never *ever* feel the warmth of him again was too acute.

"Penny?" She felt Irene's arm around her shoulder and fought against burying her face against the younger woman's silky blond hair.

"Penny . . . you've got to do something," Irene whispered.

"This isn't like me." Penny's green eyes were wide with disbelief.

"You're clever," Irene said, leading her back to the selection of antique petticoats. "You'll think of something. Now try on this blouse—and this little skirt. I know you think I'm a throwback, but sometimes shopping can break the ice . . . in your heart. Besides, with that tiny waist of yours and that willowy body, you'll look gorgeous. Come on now, please."

Penny brushed her eyes and managed to grin at Irene's pleading face. "You're anything but a throwback." She took the clothes from the little blonde.

"I know," Irene chirped as she followed Penny into the fitting room. "I'm for women's rights and all that, but I still like pretty things, and I have been known to spend the day in bed sulking and devouring a whole box of chocolates."

Penny laughed outright. "I bet you did." Her eyes twinkled at Irene as she wriggled out of her jeans and shirt and began to slip into the fragile white lace blouse.

"Buy it!" Irene cheered when Penny stood before her, resplendent in white.

Penny stared at her image in the mirror, struck by the incongruity of her straight, shiny, sandy hair—in its no-nonsense cut—and the delicate femininity of the Victorian clothes. Beneath the skirt her long legs moved freely, and she was amazed at how comfortable the soft fabric felt against her skin. She moved her arms above her head and Irene let out a shriek of alarm.

"I want to make sure I can move in this." Penny bent over from the waist.

"Stop!" cried Irene. "These are antiques! You're not supposed to move!"

"I'm going to forget you said that." Penny tossed Irene a threatening look. "You are behaving like a throwback. I have to move. Why buy clothes I can't move in? Besides"—she demonstrated a tennis serve and then kicked up one leg—"I can move."

"You're nuts," laughed Irene, relieved that Penny was acting more like her old self.

"I guess I am," Penny said, then sighed with relief. "Irene, thanks. Next time I'm depressed I want you to take me shopping."

"Are you going to buy them?" Irene asked.

"Nope." Penny laughed at Irene's shocked expression. "They're not my style. I feel dumb in white lace."

* * *

Thanks to her lunch break with Irene the rest of the day was not as grim as the previous day. Nevertheless, she thought as she walked back to the Yacht Club around dusk, it was not exactly terrific. Joel had not been called during the afternoon, so at least she hadn't had to face the tension of avoiding him or hoping that he would seek her out. However, with only two more days of shooting before the show returned to New York, there was very little likelihood that she would return with any film of her own. That aspect of the remote was almost certain to be a dismal flop.

But Joel was another matter, and the more she thought of her conversation with Irene the more she knew the blond woman was right. She could not just let things go. After examining the progression of events that had led to his outburst, she was almost certain that his change of mood had directly resulted from her enthusiasm over her career. Was it possible that he had felt threatened by her optimism, threatened by the notion of her success? Or did he, as a veteran of the business, know so much about the negative aspects of television that he truly feared an involvement with a woman who was also in the industry?

In any case, Penny thought as she turned in at the stone pillars that marked the entrance to the New England Yacht Club, she was going to speak out. She would shower and dress and then knock on his door. If he was out for the evening, and she had cautioned herself to be prepared for that, she would leave a note asking him to please phone her if he didn't get home too late.

Her scuffed-up tennis shoes crunched on the gravel, and she was deep in thought. So deep in thought that she did not see Joel helping Tippy Malone into the front seat of his Porsche. Not until she heard the low familiar hum of his engine did she look up and then just in time to see Joel and Tippy driving off together.

Damn him! What sort of a game was he playing? She ran back to her room and threw herself red-faced and breathless on her bed. It was one thing for him to sever ties with her, but couldn't he have the decency. . . . Oh, what was she saying? He had been seeing Tippy all along, and she had been fool enough to ignore it. Or rather, she had ignored Tippy's ambiguous presence in his life whenever she wasn't being forced to deal with it. For instance, she never thought about Tippy when she and Joel were making love, when his hands were gliding over her body and. . . .

Penny bounded furiously off the bed. She'd be damned if she was going back to miserable square one. She had wasted enough time mewling and moaning over that conceited man.

She took a quick shower and emerged as angry as she had been before she stepped under the coursing hot water. She glared at herself in the steamy mirror. "Fool!" she spat out at her pinched face. This was almost her last night in Marblehead. Tomorrow night she would have to go to bed early since the call for the final day of shooting was pre-dawn. If she wanted to tie one on it would have to be tonight. And she did, oh she definitely did want to tie one on!

She dialed Irene's room, but there was no answer. No doubt Irene and Pierre were off having a fabulous time. Next she tried Faye, then one by one she tried most of the members of the staff. Everyone had already made plans for the evening.

She fought back self-pity and dressed with extreme care, as if she were preparing for an important occasion. She put mascara on her lashes and perfume behind her ears, then stopped on her way out of her room because she had no idea whatsoever where she was going.

"Fool," she cursed herself, then dashed to the phone for it had occurred to her that she would take herself to dinner, alone, to the best restaurant in Marblehead.

About half an hour later Penny arrived at La Mer and was ushered to her table by the maître d', the same man who had seated her and Joel on their first evening out. She tried out her present-tense French on him, and he smiled indulgently, replying very slowly in his native tongue.

La Mer was crowded. As she sipped her glass of white wine she told herself how lucky she was to have gotten in without a reservation, but already she knew it had been a mistake to come. Everything about the place reminded her of Joel. The resonant chords of the classical guitarist sounded mournful, the Bach prelude more like a dirge than the joyous affirmation it had been on that first night with Joel.

Halfway through her entrée she spotted Max whispering something to the maître d'. Catching his eye, she waved.

"Are you alone?" Max seemed surprised.

"You?" Penny inquired, and when Max nodded she asked him to join her.

"I need a stiff one." Max gestured for the waiter and ordered a double martini.

"Join the crowd." Penny toasted him with her white wine. "I know it's a slow way to obliterate one's senses, but I have to get home under my own steam."

"So switch to martinis," Max suggested, "and I'll steer you back to the Club."

Penny declined and watched Max guzzle his martini in record time. "The work's been going much better," she observed after Max had placed his dinner order and requested another martini.

"Ah yes." Max was wistful for a moment.

"I'm glad you joined me," Penny said. She did so like Max; despite the many times he had barked at her in the past two weeks, there was a gentleness about him that always disarmed her.

They chatted easily about the show and about the final day of shooting, which would take place on Ross Herrington's *Luscious* near a remote island some fifteen miles north of Marblehead.

"I want you in on the editing back in New York," Max volunteered. "As a matter of fact, Penny, if you want I'll turn one whole episode over to you."

"That would be great." Penny's gratitude was tinged with regret. It would be good experience to edit an entire segment, but as far as her professional goals were concerned it would be of little use. She needed to direct a major scene, to have her name appear on the credits.

"Has it been a good time for you, Penny?" Max picked aimlessly at his food and finally shoved the plate aside.

Penny shrugged. "I guess."

"I was hard on you." Max shook his head in self-disgust. "You know me I . . . well, things should be better once we get back to the city. Anyway, I'm sorry."

"It's okay." Penny felt tears spring to her eyes. "What's wrong, Max?" She realized the question had as much to do with herself as it did with him. Somehow she felt their moods were linked.

"Personal mix-ups." Max's attempt to smile was a dismal failure, and for a moment Penny thought that he too was about to dissolve in tears.

"We're quite a couple," Penny said wryly, and Max managed a feeble grin.

"My life is a mess," he said drily as the waiter returned with his fourth martini.

"I'm sorry." Penny had met Max's wife only briefly. She was a stern-faced brisk woman who appeared to be as dour and unyeilding as Max was gregarious and frantic. Penny remembered someone saying she was a teacher, and she knew they had three children because sometimes the children visited Max at the studio. The oldest child, Penny guessed, was already in college.

The conversation veered away from the personal back to the show. Max hinted that he was not looking forward to the final day of shooting and not, he said, because it didn't interest him as a director. There were other reasons, but he did not explain.

"I did something I never thought I'd do." Penny spoke without forethought.

"What's that?" Max picked up the check and waved her off when she protested. "On the company," he winked. "What did you do that you thought you wouldn't?"

"I fell in love," Penny said flatly, and Max eyed her skeptically. "With an actor."

"My God." As it dawned on Max what she was talking about, his face softened. "Joel?"

Penny nodded. "Some sucker, huh? I know how to pick them, right? Max, tell me what a fool I am. I need a good bawling out."

"Ah . . . Penny." Max reached for her hand and squeezed it warmly. "Maybe I'm going blind. I shoulda guessed. I've been so wrapped up in my own mess. But it's not going so good, huh?"

"I guess not," Penny said wearily. "I don't know what went wrong . . . I don't know. I guess he's still involved with Tippy. Maybe that's it."

"I don't think so." Max leaned forward confidentially.

"Don't think what?" Penny was suddenly alert.

"I don't think Joel is involved with Tippy." Max sounded sure of himself, but maybe, she thought, it was just the martinis speaking.

"I'm giving you advice." Max put the drink aside and took her hand again. "Joel Sanborne is one hell of a man. He needs a good woman and . . . and you . . . you're one hell of a good woman."

"Max . . ." Penny flushed and the tears came again to her eyes.

"I'm telling you they don't make them better than you two. Now you may think I'm just a drunk old hasbeen, but I'm telling you, you ought to do everything you can do to straighten out whatever has come between you and Joel." Max shook his head, and though his voice was thick with intoxication there was an authenticity to his words. "He's one in a million, Penny. Joel Sanborne is one in a million."

# CHAPTER TEN

Joel Sanborne was one in a million. Max Frost's evaluation meant a great deal, for although he was definitely not the world's finest director Penny trusted him as if he were her father. That Max's opinion of Joel corresponded to her own deep, instinctive estimation of his character was nearly cause for celebration. After all, Max had known Joel for years, had been responsible for hiring him for *Dream of Life*, had seen him through one divorce and who knew how many love affairs. If anyone could be relied upon to know the status between Tippy and Joel, Max could. Now that she thought of it, Max seemed to dote on Tippy every bit as much as Joel did.

*Why?* Penny bolted to an upright position in her bed and stared incredulously into the darkness. With so many tumultuous new emotions churning away inside of her she had been unable to ask herself, objectively, why both Max and Joel reacted to Tippy with such deep concern.

Penny hugged her knees against her chest. She had been so determined to see every gesture Joel made regarding Tippy as a threat that she had pretty much ignored the fact that Max reacted to Tippy in precisely the same way. Yet . . . she had never once suspected Max of any involvement with Tippy.

Hadn't she simply fallen into the trap of believing that a handsome man (Joel) plus a beautiful woman (Tippy) necessarily added up to only one conclusion? Love, sex . . . in any case an involvement that was cause for jealousy.

Penny squeezed her thighs more tightly against her chest. She knew so many people, men and women alike, who were so possessive and untrusting of their mates that they would not tolerate friendships with the opposite sex. One of her best friends was fond of saying that friendship between men and women was virtually impossible. She claimed that true, deep friendship would inevitably lead to bed and then, of course, friendship would not be the proper word for what they were to each other. But what sort of a world was it where men and women could only really mean one thing to each other?

Penny snuggled back down into the four-poster bed, and for the first time in two days allowed herself the luxury of remembering how it had felt to lie in Joel Sanborne's arms. His embraces had been varied and unexpected, excruciatingly tender, violently passionate. Max was right, Penny smiled sleepily. Joel was one in a million and in more ways than one.

The next morning Penny awakened refreshed and eager to greet the day. Because the final day of shooting would be a long one today's call was not until eleven, so she took advantage of the time to begin to organize her clothes and scripts for the trip back to New York. The French doors were thrown wide open, letting in the sweet, early-morning chirping of the little birds as they darted on and off her terrace in search of crumbs. Penny hummed lightly to herself. Through the wall that separated her room from Joel's she heard the shower start, and she smiled, convinced that they would be able to work through their problems. Theirs was not simply one of those brief affairs that remotes seemed to propagate.

But when would be the best time to talk to him? Penny paused in the midst of packing and her stomach quivered with nervousness. Well, of course she was going to be nervous, but that was no excuse for not doing something. Still, she rationalized, morning was probably not the best time for a long talk. Probably the best time would be after work, maybe over a drink in the bar or walking along the beach below.

Damned if she wasn't getting cold feet! Timing was so important. She wadded up soiled lingerie and stuffed it in a corner of her suitcase. At least she had made a fair dent in the packing ordeal. Why did one's clothes seem to multiply in direct proportion to the number of days one spent away from home?

Penny slipped into her bikini and, grabbing a towel and the remaining scripts, headed for the pool.

"Hey, Pen!" Archie Marshall was seated under one of the cheery yellow umbrellas. She waved at him, tossed her towel aside, and dived smoothly into the water. After several laps she pulled herself gasping out of the pool. Archie was smiling down at her, holding her towel.

"Thanks." She took the towel dubiously and began rubbing herself vigorously.

"We should have this weather tomorrow when we're out on the boat," Archie said with a smile. "I ordered coffee for you." He gestured to his table, which was shaded by the umbrella.

Penny hesitated for a moment, then recalling the lecture she had given herself only last night she grinned at Archie and joined him.

"Melon?" He insisted on sharing his fare with her.

"Nothing like fresh fruit for breakfast." She reached for one of the plump red strawberries and popped it in her mouth.

"Jan's coming tonight," Archie announced, and Penny felt all of her reservations melting away.

"Great!" she enthused. "She'll be here for the big party tomorrow night then?"

Archie nodded warmly. He seemed more like the old easygoing, likable Archie. The Archie she had known in New York. Odd, she thought, how people could take on different colors in new surroundings. It was almost impossible now to believe that he had been capable of making matters so difficult for her.

135

"We're going to take a week and drive up to Maine." He offered Penny one of the buttery hot croissants which were wrapped in a crisp white linen napkin. "Jan's mother's staying with the girls. You know . . . it's hard being married for a long time."

Penny's mouth twitched in an amused smile, and she glanced knowingly at Archie. He scratched his blond hair as his face flushed slightly at his oblique confession.

"I'll bet it is hard." Penny munched the croissant pensively. "How long have you and Jan been married?"

Archie grimaced dramatically. "Would you believe twenty years?"

"No!" Penny exclaimed. "That long?"

Archie nodded and there was a hint of pride in his grin as he continued. "We have our ups and downs but . . . when it comes right down to it . . . I can't imagine my life without her."

Penny felt a lump of sentiment rise in her throat. Was it possible that she could feel the same way about Joel in so short a time? It was true that she couldn't imagine her life without him. Would it be true in twenty years?

She looked steadily at Archie. "That's quite an accomplishment in this day and age. Twenty years is long."

"At times like this"—Archie's blue eyes took on an unexpectedly naïve glimmer—"it doesn't seem long. Sometimes it seems like we just met. Would you believe I can't wait to see her . . . that I'm actually a little nervous?"

Penny and Archie laughed together, and as Penny reached to pour herself another cup of coffee Joel sauntered over wearing his navy swimming trunks.

"Who laughs this early in the morning?" Joel's smile was too broad, his voice filled with a forced gusto.

"Hey, Joel." Archie pulled out the extra chair. "Try these blueberries."

Joel slid into the chair and stretched his long legs off to the side of the table. He smiled pleasantly at Penny. "You look fetching."

His dark eyes fastened for a moment on the scant bikini top, and Penny felt a rush of pleasure as her nipples turned hard beneath the flimsy fabric.

"Thanks." She looked away from him, her heart racing. He seemed like his old self . . . charming, friendly, even flirtatious.

"So . . ." Joel addressed Archie as he helped himself to the last croissant. "I hear you're going on a vacation at the end of this fiasco. You lucky dog."

"A little fishing," gloated Archie, "a little lobster on the deserted rocky beaches of Maine."

Penny glanced sideways at Joel. The mention of lobster and rocky beaches had sent a tingle of desire through her body. But Joel gave no indication that the remark had fazed him; certainly it had not had the same jolting effect on him as it had on Penny. He and Archie continued chatting about life in the great north woods while Penny picked up the morning newspaper and tried to concentrate on the editorial.

"And you . . . ?" Joel tapped the newspaper lightly to get her attention.

"What?" Her mouth twitched uneasily as her eyes met his.

"I wondered"—he looked at her enigmatically—"what you were doing?"

Penny stared at him uncomprehendingly.

"When we leave Marblehead," he clarified with a patient smile.

He was speaking to her as if they were total strangers. Yes, he was friendly, charming, and even flirtatious, but something was missing. It was as if he was trying not to see her, as if he were playing a scene.

"Back to New York." Her eyes searched his for a sign, and for a moment, just a brief instant, a glimmer of true recognition crossed his face.

"No trips to the beach over Labor Day weekend?" He laughed and again his laughter rang false to her.

"No." She did not try to hide her disappointment. Her gamin face reflected it all—the dejection as well as her feelings for him.

Her large green eyes articulated her confusion more eloquently than words could have ever done, and when he turned away abruptly she knew that he had read her correctly.

"You'll be awfully hot in New York over Labor Day." Joel stood up, leaving the half-finished croissant on his plate. "Won't she, Arch?"

"Oh . . . yes." Archie looked up from his section of the paper. He had completely missed the silent innuendos that had passed between Joel and Penny.

Penny watched Joel dive into the pool with a numb, sinking feeling. It was not going to be as easy as she had imagined. He had armed himself against her, and his new tack was not to ignore her as he had done over the past two days but to almost court her with an armour of phony charm and friendliness. It was the behavior he reserved for fans who besieged him.

"What time is it?" Penny asked Archie, who was gathering up his towel and newspaper.

"Time to put pleasure aside," Archie joshed, "and go to the salt mines."

Penny threw her towel over her shoulder and sat on the edge of the pool with her feet dangling in the water. She watched Joel moving rapidly through the water and counted twenty laps before she pulled herself to her feet and went inside her room to get ready to go to work.

The show was shooting in a dank, wooded area that seemed to be swarming with mosquitoes. An almost celestial light filtered through the tall pines, and the heavy, fecund scent of pine needles and moist moss filled the air. These deeply sensual, junglelike surroundings worked almost like an aphrodisiac on Penny. When she wasn't taking notes for Max or involved in some other work-oriented task, she found herself sprawled on the thickly carpeted forest floor, staring in a kind of stupor at the majestic pines. Even the pesky mosquitoes could not ruin the profound beauty of the spot.

She had forgone lunch to retreat to a solitary glade where deep

138

shadows formed magically mysterious pockets. The work was running smoothly, and she had been pleasantly surprised to find that Max had suffered no ill effects from his martini splurge the night before. In fact Max had seemed almost exuberant, and Tippy, oddly enough, was more like her usual, vital self.

Penny lay on her back with her arms thrown wide above her head and her jeaned legs spread on the cushiony pine needle floor. Tippy had even played a joke on Archie in one of the takes, and everyone had had a good laugh. That, thought Penny, was more like Tippy, who was usually the darling of the technical crew because of her infectious sense of humor. Perhaps it was only because the remote was nearing conclusion, but there was suddenly an all-pervasive togetherness and closeness among everyone. Penny closed her eyes, feeling as though she had been drugged. Even the rift between her and Archie had undergone a totally unexpected turn for the good.

She sighed deeply and felt her limbs melt into the damp earth. How beautiful these woods were, she thought, and how like a balm they were to her. Thoughts of Joel and what lay ahead held no dread. Surrounded by such grandeur her soul felt confident and at peace.

She must have dozed. The snap of a twig or crackle of a leaf awakened her, and she opened her eyes to see Joel standing over her. He was wearing the snug-fitting khaki shorts and safari jacket that were Buck Handlin's attire for the scenes they were shooting today. Still under the influence of the forest's aphrodisia she fastened her inquisitive green eyes on his large, sinewy thighs, noting that slight indentation on the outer thigh, recalling how it had felt beneath the palm of her inquiring hand.

There was no mistaking the look in his eyes as he gazed down at her. However much he had wanted to hide from her earlier in the day, he was unable to keep up the pretense of indifference after finding her so vulnerable and at peace in these hauntingly lovely surroundings.

"Everyone is looking for you," he said gruffly.

Penny swallowed back the desire and blinked her eyes. She knew she had to rouse herself but was reluctant to let the moment end.

"You fell asleep." Joel raised his eyes to the tall pines and then looked back at her. He too appeared to be in no hurry to break the spell.

"Yes." Penny's voice was breathless.

He bent down beside her, his face only inches from hers, his eyes dark and penetrating. He placed her hand on his bare thigh, then moved it slowly so that she would understand precisely how he had been affected.

Penny closed her eyes and let out a low moan.

"You see what you do to me." Joel breathed hotly against her cheek as his hand ran along her arm creating warm, undulating waves in her entire body.

"Yes," she gasped as his mouth crushed against hers and she felt herself spiraling headlong into the unknown. It was so easy to fall. With him it was all too easy. Was that wrong, she wondered dimly.

"We can't." He pulled her fully clothed body against him and moved against her. The fabrics separating their flesh seemed only a minor intrusion as their two bodies drew together almost involuntarily, as if each were the perfect magnet to the other.

"I know," she groaned as her arms wrapped around his waist, urging him on. Beneath her clothes she felt the gush of passion, and sensing her arousal Joel unbuttoned her blouse and eased one breast toward his famished mouth.

"The others were sure you'd gone back to the trucks. . . . I knew better." He flicked his tongue and the rosy bud stiffened.

"Yes," she crooned as his hand fumbled with the button on her blue jeans then slid onto her tight stomach until she cried out.

Insistently his hand plunged lower, searching out the spot that made her nearly wild with desire. She wriggled enthusiastically until he moaned. "Is this crazy?" He pressed his lips against her neck, and she felt his teeth nibbling lightly. He plunged his hand deeper, and with each stroke she felt his hunger for her grow.

Suddenly he pulled away from her. He sat tensely next to her, listening. His breath was coming in short dry gasps, and he moved his hand to his forehead to brush away the beads of perspiration that had formed there.

Faintly Penny heard someone calling her name, and she scrambled to her feet and made herself presentable as Joel began to move in the direction of Johnny Robello's voice.

"Are you okay?" He stopped and turned back to look at her with solemn eyes.

She nodded mutely, still shaky, still unable to put the moment in perspective. He reached for her hand and led her through the trees, and once they reached Robello and the others he dropped her hand.

"I found her." He smiled easily. "She was sleeping." And that was all he said.

Penny had hoped to be able to arrange for a time for them to talk before they left the idyllic location, but as luck would have it, Joel had finished working earlier and she had remained behind to complete some long shots of Archie and the four-wheel drive. By the time she arrived back at the Yacht Club there was no question what her first priority was. There was no way she could talk to him until she had showered and changed and felt a bit more human.

As she opened the door to her room she noted the Do Not Disturb sign on Joel's door and smiled. Probably he was taking his usual nap before dinner. It was a habit of which she approved and indulged in herself.

It was only six o'clock by the digital clock. Penny stripped out of her filthy work clothes and padded naked into the bathroom. She grinned at her dirt-streaked face, then stepped into the steaming shower. Even though they had started filming later in the day, they had, as Max predicted, finished early. They were actually coming in on schedule despite all of the setbacks.

141

Penny scrubbed herself vigorously with the loofah sponge and the fresh, minty bath gel. Joel loved her! Not only had he declared himself after their night on board the *Luscious,* the look in his eye today had confirmed all of her instinctive feelings. Of course, she smiled as she raised her face to the shower head, it would be easier if he would simply phone and say "Let's have dinner." She would naturally prefer that he make the first move, but because of their encounter in the forest she was determined to persevere.

In case he was napping she did not want to phone him, so with a towel wrapped around her wet hair, she peeked outside the door. The Do Not Disturb sign was still in place. She switched on some low music and proceeded with her preparations, drying her hair until it gleamed and putting a light lotion on her rosy, tanned skin. She slipped into the gray linen slacks and a short-sleeved white cotton blouse that accentuated her healthy glow. It was after seven. She peeked out the door again. The Do Not Disturb sign had been removed.

Experiencing a last-minute attack of nerves, she retreated back into her room. In high school she had always dreaded any event where the girls had to invite the boys. Inevitably she had put off asking anyone until it was too late. Only once before Joel had she summoned up the courage to ask out a member of the opposite sex.

"Silly," she scolded herself, but she stood for several minutes inside her room with her hand hovering over the doorknob. Perhaps she should phone first?

No, she shook her head. If he was still of a mind to retreat from her, he would have an easier job doing it over the phone. She wanted to confront him directly.

But what would she say? Well . . . first off she would tell him that whatever decision he made about his career would have nothing to do with the way she felt about him. She was not in love with a television star or with a man who happened to earn an enormous amount of money. No matter what he did she would love him. And . . . as far as her career was concerned, he needn't feel threatened—though perhaps that was too direct a way of phrasing it.

As she rehearsed her part silently, she cringed. Inside her head the words sounded as dry and unfeeling as a corporate lawyer's plea for amalgamation. She opened the door to her room abruptly and before she could come up with any more excuses she was knocking on his door.

# CHAPTER ELEVEN

At first there was no answer and she was about to retreat when she heard him turning the lock.

"Hi." She tried unsuccessfully to smile.

"Hi . . ." He was still wearing his khaki shorts, but he had removed his shirt and his shoes and socks. He shifted uneasily and his expression was defenseless, almost guilty.

"Who is it?" Tippy's voice came from the corner of his room where Penny knew the bed to be.

Penny's head jerked involuntarily toward the sound of the other woman's voice.

"Just Penny," she heard her voice reply evenly as her eyes slowly took in Tippy's tousled hair, her diminutive, curvacious body clad only in a colorful silk Japanese kimono as she lounged seductively on Joel's bed.

"You've finished then?" Tippy coughed distastefully as she smashed out her cigarette in the ashtray on the bedside table.

"Yes." Penny felt her spine stiffen. Her eyes returned to Joel's face. "I just wanted to let you know that we'll be shooting out of sequence tomorrow. We'll be doing the third scene first, then the second. From that point on everything will be in sequence. That's, uh . . . the scene with all the extras first."

"Is that a change?" piped Tippy.

Penny paused and drew herself up to her full height as she stared placidly into Joel's confused face. She had no idea at all what she had said or if it had made any sense. She assumed from his expression, however, that she had been convincing, and Tippy's question also led her to believe that she had survived with her dignity intact.

"Yes, it's a change." She lowered her eyes and walked away.

"Thanks," she heard Joel call after her, and his voice sounded hollow, like the voice of someone in a dream.

The heels of her sandals resounded on the cement walk that bordered the now deserted pool. She stared blankly into the deep blue water with a detached feeling, then as if in a dream, she walked across the velvety lawn. The terrace dining room was humming with activity. Almost every table was taken, she noted with great interest. Faye and Johnny Robello were having dinner together. She smiled, waved, and continued walking.

She entered the bar with its whirring white ceiling fans and white wicker furniture. The drinking crowd had already left to go to dinner, and except for two couples at tables the bar was deserted. Without deciding to do so she perched herself on one of the high barstools and ordered a martini from the bartender.

Her fingers closed around the surface of the chilled glass that the bartender had placed in front of her. Had she said she wanted it on the rocks? She couldn't remember. She raised her glass to her lips and sipped, placed the glass back on the old Victorian bar, and waited.

What was she feeling? Calm. Wasn't she too calm? Her mind went back to Tippy's body curled comfortably on Joel's bed. Had the bed been made or unmade? Odd that that detail had escaped her scrutiny. She took another sip of the martini and waited.

Why had Tippy been in his room? Why had he placed a Do Not Disturb sign on his door when clearly he had not been taking a nap? What did it mean?

She took a shallow sip of the frigid drink and waited for the emotional onslaught to hit her. She cocked her head slightly as if she might even be able to hear the echo of self-recrimination, her own harsh words telling her what a fool she had been. But there was nothing. Surely she felt something. She toyed with the martini glass and her green eyes were pensive.

Joel had been dismayed at her unexpected appearance. It was the first time she had ever seen him at a total loss. She frowned hard. Why didn't she feel rejected, humiliated, angry?

She finished the martini, cautiously waiting for her self-image to crumble. A slow smile parted her full lips as she realized that that was not going to happen. Suddenly she felt positively giddy with a new sense of power over herself. Yes, Tippy had been sprawled on Joel's bed clad in a flimsy robe. Yes, Joel had been in bare feet without a shirt on. Yes, they had been together. Only—and now her smile spread to a grin—she felt not one iota of jealousy or concern. There was an explanation for what seemed on the surface to be a questionable, compromising situation. If she really wanted to understand what was going on between Tippy and Joel she would be able to find out.

"A glass of soda water with lime," she said, waving at the bartender. She had not misunderstood the situation, had not jumped to conclusions. Nothing had changed, and she was still going to find the opportunity to speak with Joel privately.

No sooner had those thoughts passed through her mind than she felt his presence on the barstool next to her.

"Hi," he said tightly, and when she looked at him his eyes were worried.

"Don't worry." She tried to stifle the bubble of laughter rising in her throat. His dark eyes widened.

"I wanted to explain," he began earnestly, but she placed her hand on his and interrupted him.

"Only if you want to," she said. "Only if you can."

Joel looked at her with the same baffled expression. "You . . . you're not upset?"

Finally Penny could not hold back a spurt of laughter. "I'm not," she confessed. "Honestly, I can't believe I'm not. I've been pretty miserable for the past two days. I mean, today is the first time . . ."

"It must have looked pretty incriminating." Joel studied her incredulously.

"I know," Penny said with an amazed voice. "But . . . I know you wouldn't do a thing like that."

"Like what?" He leaned into her intently.

"Only a cad—or a very neurotic person—would sleep with one woman and then bring another woman in the same circle of friends to his room. That's game playing," she went on, "and you're too good for that. You don't have time for that."

Joel nodded in mute agreement.

"Anyway"—the smile left her face and she met his eyes with a new sense of urgency—"I believed you when you said you loved me. You're not a careless person. You have too much sensitivity, too much . . . honor to throw those words around."

Joel shook his head in awe. His dark eyes were limpid as he gently took her chin and tilted it up toward his lips.

"I do love you." His eyes were glistening.

"And I love you." Penny's voice was barely audible. Joel's lips brushed hers lightly, then he leaned back to regard her with an admiring smile.

"You sure know how to surprise a guy." He shook his head.

"I surprised myself," Penny said, then took a gulp of the soda water.

"You really trust me?" Joel questioned with a note of disbelief. Then he answered his own question. "You really do."

"In this instance." Penny met his eyes with a mischievous grin.

He reached for her glass and took a thirsty sip. "Soda water?"

Penny nodded. "I had a martini first. It seemed like the proper response. You know, go straight to the bar and drown your sorrows."

"Or get up enough nerve to say what you *really* think," Joel added thoughtfully. "But you say what you really think when you're cold sober."

"There are some people," Penny observed wryly, "who consider that an annoying trait."

"Not me." Joel took her hand and kissed it. "Life is ambiguous enough. One does not need ambiguity from one's . . ."

Penny's heart skipped a beat, and she picked up the glass of soda water to cover her excitement. What had he been going to say? One's . . . what? What was she to him?

"I know this is a pretty trite compliment," he said ruefully, "but I've, honest to God, never met anyone like you."

"Then we're even," said Penny, then she laughed, adding, "because I have never met anyone like you either."

"I'm sorry for behaving so stupidly after we came back from Concord. Going on and on about quitting the show, somehow trying to put the blame on you. I wanted to explain . . . several times I started to call you." Joel broke off with a shrug.

"It's hard to take the first step," Penny offered sympathetically.

"Is that what you were doing tonight when you came to my room?" he asked.

Penny nodded.

"Timing." He brushed the back of his hand lightly along her cheek. "We're going to work it out, you know. We really are. We have a rare thing going here . . . it would be a shame to muck it up."

Penny's eyes welled up and several large tears spilled out.

"Hey!" Joel dug in his pocket for a handkerchief and dabbed at her eyes. "I don't ever want to make you cry."

"I'm crying with happiness." Penny was appalled at the tears that were now spilling out even as she was laughing.

"One of a kind," Joel reiterated two hours later as they lingered over after-dinner coffee on the terrace. "A gal who can walk in on her man and see a sexy dame like Tippy on his bed and not jump to the wrong conclusion is one of a kind. Do we dare order a bottle of champagne to celebrate?"

Penny wrinkled her nose and looked dubious.

"A bottle of vintage Crystal? Does that whet your appetite?" Joel chuckled seductively.

"I don't know what Crystal is," Penny said directly. "Does that count as a strike against me?"

Beneath the table Joel's hand caressed the curve of her hip, and when she flushed in reaction he laughed. "No. No strikes against you. It just means I shall have to teach you!" He squinted lasciviously at her as he removed his hand from her thigh.

"You can teach me anytime," Penny replied in a whisper. It positively amazed her that the very touch of his hand sent the blood throbbing and thundering to her very core. She glanced quickly at her watch then laughed as she caught him looking at her with an amused twinkle in his eyes.

"Always worrying about time and business," he teased.

"I think it might be a little late for champagne. I wouldn't want to step on board the *Luscious* at six in the morning with a champagne hangover."

Joel smiled. "You have a point. Nothing is as bad as a champagne hangover. So . . . how about another cognac?"

Penny shoved her glasses down on her nose and peered at him like an old-fashioned schoolmarm. "Do you know your lines for tomorrow?"

"As a matter of fact," boasted Joel, "I have a photographic mind. One glance at the script and the words are imprinted in my cerebellum."

"I've noticed you're pretty fast," Penny quipped.

"Yes," he said with a silly leer, "very. So what do you think? Another cognac as we fill our lungs full of sea air and honeysuckle?"

"I'll give you a choice," said Penny playfully. "We can either sit here on the terrace sniffing honeysuckle and sipping cognac or—"

"Or what?" Joel jumped in with a glint in his eye.

"Or . . . we can return to your room . . . or mine . . . and opt for something a little more athletic."

149

"You devil!" Joel chuckled with delight. "You really are an amazing creature."

Penny pressed her lips together primly. "It is nine twenty-five and twenty seconds. If we step on it we can reach our destination by nine thirty."

Joel laughed as he reached in his pocket and threw his credit card down on the table. "No choice." He glanced at her. "The day I choose cognac and honeysuckle over making love to you will never come."

Penny blushed. "Promises, promises." She stood up from the table, and as Joel dealt with the waiter her eyes moved around the flower-filled terrace with a sense of nostalgia. This was really the last night. Tomorrow night there would be a big bash, so this was really the last, quiet night in these elegant surroundings. How she had grown to love this place.

As they strolled across the spongy green lawn to their rooms, Penny leaned into Joel's sinewy body feeling more supremely at peace than she had ever felt before. What passed between them as they walked, his arm tight around her waist, hers around his, was as magical as the silver light that shimmered through the high cumulus clouds as they passed over the waxing moon.

"This has to be the most romantic spot in the world," she sighed as she inserted her key in the lock.

Joel followed her inside the room and watched her fondly as she opened the doors to the terrace to let the night sea breeze waft through.

"I was so mad," she remarked, "when I first discovered you were next door."

Joel sat down on the edge of the bed and took off his shoes. "Well, you certainly didn't let on," he joked.

"I was sure that you were arranging for your remote amusement." Penny's pulse accelerated as he began to unbutton his shirt.

"And would it have been so bad if I had?" he queried as he removed his white shirt and hung it carefully on a hanger.

150

Penny watched as he smoothed the wrinkles out of his shirt before placing it inside the armoire next to her clothes. The gesture was somehow shockingly intimate. His shirt next to her clothes, the two of them talking almost casually as they prepared for bed—it was so easy!

"I thought so at the time," she said finally. She turned away from him and unzipped the gray linen slacks. She removed the slacks with the slightest hesitation, and as she pressed the creases together she turned to see him smiling at her.

"We're both very neat people," he laughed. "I see you crease your trousers too."

Penny's stomach did a delicious turn at the seductive tone that had come into his low baritone. She crossed to the armoire and reached for a hanger. She could feel him staring at her bare legs, at the scant bikini panties. She removed her blouse and hung it on the same hanger with her gray linen slacks. She paused breathlessly, more overcome by a surge of desire than by a sense of modesty. Her breasts were firm and lush beneath the lacy bra, and they rose and fell in heightened anticipation.

Just as she was about to bend forward to remove the bra and slip into her robe, she felt his cool hand against her waist. He turned her around until she was facing him. He was wearing only a pair of pale blue boxer shorts. Standing eye to eye with him like this with the gentle breeze caressing their bodies, Penny felt near to bursting with joy.

"You are beautiful." Joel touched her forehead then slowly traced the outline of her face as if to memorize it. His hand moved tenderly to the curve of her long, slender neck then out to her smooth, tanned shoulders and back to her throat.

"When we get back to New York," he said thickly, "we will spend days like this."

"Yes." Penny's green eyes were dreamy. This was the first time he had mentioned a future and to have it named . . . *when we get back to New York* . . . made the evening even more perfect.

"In my apartment"—his hand moved slowly to where her breasts spilled appealingly from under their lacy confinement—

151

"we will open all the windows and lie together facing the river. I'm on the twelfth floor." His eyes roamed her face and his voice was even more sultry as his hand molded itself against her right breast.

"I can see all the way to the George Washington Bridge. We'll make love all day. No Max, no early-morning calls, no responsibilities . . . just the two of us."

"I accept," Penny articulated with some difficulty as Joel reached around her lithe body and unfastened her bra.

As he took one rosy nipple between his thumb and forefinger, Penny let out a moan of delight that seemed to arouse him even more.

"I want to go slow with you, Penny," he crooned against her ear, "but it is very difficult."

He swept her up in his arms and carried her over to the four-poster bed where he drew back the lacy coverlet before laying her down on the cool white sheets. Her eyes half-closed with sultry longing as she stared up at him, taking in the extraordinary wealth of his masculinity as he stripped out of his shorts.

"You too." Her full lips melted into a passionate smile. "You are beautiful too."

Then suddenly it was as if a cataclysmic desire burst uncontrollably out of him, and the painstakingly deliberate prelude segued into a torrent as he ripped off the remaining barrier and plunged smoothly into her.

The moans that shook his huge body as he clung to her drove her higher and higher until she felt she had entered some new, faraway realm. She might never return. The thought crossed like fire through her mind, but it held no threat as her arms wrapped firmly around him and she goaded him on and on with her newly discovered power.

The wild, tumultuous currents he forced into her were welcomed with ecstatic cries. It seemed they both were of a single mind, that the two days of misunderstandings followed by their brief encounter earlier that day in the forest had whipped their passion to a frenzy. Vaguely it occurred to Penny that what was happening between them was almost ruthless in its intensity. His hands demanded untiring responses from her trembling body, but she was glad to give them to him. She dug her fingers into his flanks, and sensing his desire to alter their position she surrendered to his rocking motion. Together they rolled over until she was gazing down at him. His forehead was damp, his eyes shut so that she beheld for the first time the thick fringe of dark lashes. She moved very slowly against him, delighting in the pleasurable half-smile that formed on his lips. How she loved to please him, she thought. She wanted to give herself to him completely, like a precious gem. As she varied the thrusts of her body she was gratified by a sudden wild-eyed look of explosive surrender that made him cry out.

When he was spent, his expression once again peaceful and smiling, his eyes closed, Penny kissed his damp lids gently.

"We should sleep." He forced his eyes open and looked at her.

She put her chin on her hands and with her elbows resting lightly on his chest she studied him. "I know."

Joel's eyes drooped, but he opened them again after a moment. He drew her to him in a light, chaste kiss, then gently easing her off him he rolled over on his back and folded his arms thoughtfully beneath his head.

Penny glanced at the digital clock. "If we go to sleep now we still have a fair shot at being reasonably ambulatory tomorrow."

"Yes," Joel agreed with a pensive smile.

But they made no move to turn out the lights or set the alarm. Penny propped herself up on her elbows and examined a lock of his black hair intently as if she had never encountered a lock of hair before.

He caressed her shoulder lightly with his fingers and they were silent for a moment.

"About Tippy . . ." Joel studied the ceiling of her room with the same intensity she reserved for his hair.

"You don't have to—" Penny began.

"I want to," Joel interjected. "But I can't."

153

"I know you would explain if you could." Penny released the lock of dark hair and kissed him lightly on the earlobe.

"She's under a hell of a lot of pressure," Joel said slowly, and Penny leaned back on her pillows and studied his sober profile. He looked like an Indian god . . . so dark and almost stern-looking even in this relaxed state. There was a majesty about him. Yes, he should play parts like Macbeth . . . kings and princes. She wanted to tell him.

"I figured she was," Penny offered.

Joel turned and smiled softly at her. "She likes you."

"You mentioned me?" Penny's eyes glistened.

"Of course," Joel looked at her lovingly. "She told me I was a fool if I didn't follow you right away."

"Tippy said that?" Penny asked in an astounded voice.

"She's of the belief that I always choose the wrong kind of women." Joel gave her a reflective smile.

Penny nodded. This was the most open he had ever been with her. As always, whenever he did open up and speak honestly she found her esteem for him growing by leaps and bounds. It was the real Joel Sanborne who intrigued her.

"My ex-wife was . . ." He broke off hesitantly. "Do you want to hear this?"

Penny bobbed her head up and down. It did not occur to her that it was the least bit unnatural to be lying naked on a bed having a heart to heart conversation with a man who, until only two weeks ago, she had believed to be nothing less than a chauvinistic ogre.

"She's an actress . . . a good one. Monica Lawrence. You might have heard of her."

"Of course." Penny's eyes flew open. Monica Lawrence had made the big move from daytime television to films and was currently something of a smash in Hollywood. She was extraordinarily gorgeous—a young Sophia Loren. For an instant she felt a tug of insecurity at the idea of being compared to Monica Lawrence.

"Anyway," Joel went on, "there was a lot of competition

154

between Monica and me. She resented every job I got and I, unfortunately, did not react any better to her success."

Penny waited for him to continue, but he had apparently concluded his explanation.

"Do you . . . do you still love her?" Immediately Penny wondered why she needed to ask the question.

"No." Joel did not hesitate. He placed his forefinger firmly on the tip of her nose. "I love you."

"I'm glad." Penny fell against him, kissing his face all over, rubbing her cheek against the abrasive stubble of his beard.

"You're not still friends with her?" she asked, still kissing him.

Joel grasped her by the shoulders and held her away from him. "Monica and I were never friends," he said pointedly.

"But we are." Penny wondered if she would ever be able to find enough time just to stare at his extraordinary face.

"We are friends." Joel drew her close and kissed her. Their tongues swirled hungrily in each other's mouths, and that incessant desire she had for him began once again to bloom in her.

"I've got to get out of here!" Joel pulled reluctantly away from her.

Penny fell back on the pillows and watched him dress. "You're leaving me?" She pretended to pout.

"If I don't," Joel warned, "we will both be zombies in the morning."

"It's true." Penny giggled. "We can't seem to sleep together at the same time. Either you sleep and I watch you, or I sleep and you watch me."

"So in a sense"—Joel, now dressed, bent over and kissed her on the cheek—"you could say . . . we are not sleeping together."

"Good night." Penny snuggled down under the covers.

"Coffee on my terrace promptly at five." Joel bowed as he flicked off her lights. "You, me, and the birds."

As he closed the door to her room Penny smiled drowsily, and mere seconds later she was sound asleep.

## CHAPTER TWELVE

Five and a half hours' sleep and she felt positively bursting with energy. The next morning Penny sprang out of bed and ran for the shower. Early-morning calls at the studio back in New York had accustomed her to switching into what she referred to as "A.M. automatic." She prided herself on being able to get out of the apartment in less than half an hour from the moment her feet hit the bedroom floor. Her morning ablutions required no thought whatsoever. She slipped into her jeans while her body was still moist from the shower, pulled a long-sleeved white T-shirt over her head, jammed on her sneakers without socks, grabbed her script bag, purse, one of her swimming suits (in case there was a moment for a dip during the day), and rushed out into the dark, dewy morning.

Several birds were chirping but, Penny noted with a smile as she stood in front of Joel's door, only several.

She knocked lightly, then when there was no answer she pounded. Still there was no answer, and even when she pounded as hard as she could without waking up the guests who were sleeping in the next bungalow, there was no reply.

Perplexed, she went back inside her room and picked up the phone. She drummed her fingers on the receiver as she waited for the desk clerk to pick up. No doubt he had fallen asleep on the job. She slammed down the receiver and went outside to her terrace.

"Hey!" she hissed through the thick vines that covered the trellis separating her room from Joel's. "Joel! Joel! Wake up!"

After several tries she heard a groan of recognition as he stumbled out on his terrace. Thank God he had slept with the French doors open.

"It's open," he called drowsily. "I'll be in the shower. Just come on in and. . . . Could you call for coffee?"

Penny grinned at the sound of his sleepy voice. She managed to arouse the desk clerk and order coffee, then she let herself into Joel's room.

"Sleepyhead." She smiled as he emerged from the shower, skimpily wrapped in a towel. Dawn was just beginning to break, and below them the calm sea reflected a myriad of muted violet hues.

Joel stumbled over to a chair and gratefully accepted the cup of coffee she held out for him.

"It's a good thing Max arranged for the kitchen to provide us early birds with coffee," she said.

"Mmmm," Joel groaned as he sipped the scalding liquid.

"Did you sleep well?" Penny piped.

"Mmmm." Joel nodded and blinked his eyes as if he still was not altogether certain where he was and what was going on.

Penny resisted the urge to giggle at his groggy manner. Usually he was so vital, so incredibly energetic and powerful that it amused her to see him so . . . out of it. It was almost as if he were another person. She smiled to herself. Even this early-morning characteristic of his endeared him to her.

She left him in peace, knowing he was having a difficult enough time sipping his coffee; to expect him to converse would be ridiculous. She moved to the edge of the terrace and watched the streaks in the eastern sky change from silvery violets to pale rose and gradually, as the fiery ball appeared above the horizon, to a collage of flamboyant ribbons of crimson and orange.

"I love a sunrise," she said, turning to him eagerly.

"Mmmm," he groaned as he struggled to his feet to come and stand beside her.

She leaned into him as he continued to sip his coffee. He smelled soapy clean like a scrubbed little kid. She twisted to look up at him. He even looked like a confused little kid.

"Why are you laughing at me?" He noticed her looking, but she shook her head, her eyes sparkling.

"We'd better go." She took his hand and led him back inside, locking the French doors behind her. "I can see you need supervision in the morning."

Joel nodded mutely and watched her gather up his script and his jacket. "Is that what you're wearing for work today?" she asked, and when he shook his head no she proceeded to elicit the necessary information from him. She located his swimming suit, towel, and the two changes of clothes he would need for the filming, and only then did he nod his approval and hold the door open for her.

As they approached his car Penny stole a glance at him as he walked silently at her side. He was never this quiet.

"Would you like me to drive?" she asked.

"Sure." He felt in several pockets before he located the keys to the Porsche.

Penny slid behind the wheel, suddenly nervous about driving such a fancy vehicle. How long had it been since she'd driven a stick shift? She chewed her lower lip anxiously as she slipped the key in the ignition. The engine rumbled to a start, and she shifted into first and they made a reasonably smooth start.

By the time they turned onto the coast road that ran along the ocean and would lead them to the marina where the *Luscious* was waiting, she felt confident. The top of the car was down, and her hair was flapping out behind her ears. It was an incredibly beautiful day, pristine and cloudless.

"Ho hum." Joel leaned his head back and closed his eyes.

Penny glanced momentarily away from the curvy road and smiled at him. She was more certain than ever that they were absolutely suited for each other.

And what did that mean, she asked herself. She had never intended to fall in love . . . at least not for a very long time. And yet now that it had happened to her and she felt in every part of her mind and body how right it was, there seemed to be no alternative. She wanted to marry this man.

The thought stunned her and she swerved slightly as they rounded a curve. Marry? Marry Joel Sanborne? Well, of course, that was where it was leading in her mind. But what about his?

He had mentioned his apartment in New York. He wanted her to go there, to be with him there. But that was hardly a proposal.

Easy girl, she told herself, but the idea of marrying him had set off a new chain reaction. He had said he didn't want to rush, that he wanted to go slow. Maybe that was what he had meant. Anyway, it was ridiculous to think of marrying someone you had only just begun to know. She had always been in favor of lengthy engagements, of knowing a person for a long, long time before making any permanent commitment. She had twice tried to talk friends out of marrying men they had known only briefly. What on earth had happened to good old sensible Penny Phillips?

An amused smile played on her mouth as she thought of all her humorless protestations about not wanting to get married until she was at least in her early thirties. When it came right down to it she had really always considered herself immune from the sort of all-consuming love she felt for Joel Sanborne.

She shoved the sunglasses up on her nose and pressed her foot down on the accelerator. There was no one else on the road. Probably the van with the technical equipment had driven out even earlier, and Max himself was probably already setting things up. She watched the speedometer climb and thrilled at the power of the engine. It was like Joel, she thought—tight, smooth, hard, and capable of exhilarating speed.

She was pleased with her driving expertise but, she reminded herself, she had better slow down. How great it would be if she and Joel could drive somewhere together . . . somewhere far like across the United States on a long camping haul. Or they could fly to France and rent a car and drive around to all of his favorite spots. Just drive and drive and drive. Penny smiled, indulging in all sorts of fantasies for their future.

After she had parked the Porsche in the reserved spot at the marina she turned to Joel, expecting to see him sleeping. Instead he was grinning at her with a devilish glint in his eye.

"Lead foot," he said, shaking his finger at her.

"You were awake?" she gasped.

"Seventy-five miles an hour on a mediocre road." Joel raised a heavy eyebrow.

Penny grimaced, but before she could apologize Joel began to shake with laughter.

"I never would have guessed that of you." He attacked her ribs, tickling her. "Little miss serious straight-faced, always-be-to-work-on-time. Not only"—he leaned into her ear—"is she an insatiable lioness in the sack, she is a veritable menace on the road!"

"You weren't asleep at all." Penny wriggled away from him, giggling. "Were you even that groggy back in your room?"

Joel shook his head with a smile. "It was all an act . . . except for oversleeping and the first cup of coffee."

"And all the while I was organizing you and getting you out of your room you were letting me . . . ?"

"That's right." Joel chuckled. "Oh, you were so busy. You must have wondered how I ever got along without you."

"I did!" Penny burst into laughter. "I did! I wondered how you'd managed without someone to look after you."

"I fooled you." Joel leaped out of the car and threw open the door for her. He held out his hand, and she handed him the keys to the Porsche.

"Actually"—his eyes danced—"you are a pretty good driver."

"And you"—she laced her fingers through his—"are a pretty good actor."

"Why did you come so early, anyway?" Penny asked as their

160

sneakers slapped against the rickety dock. "You didn't have to be here until later."

"I know." Joel linked his arm through hers. "But I'm a man of my word. I wasn't really thinking clearly last night when I told you to knock on my door this morning. But the die was cast, and it hardly seemed fair for me to keep you up late last night and then indulge in an additional hour's sleep the next morning."

"You're a decent chap after all," Penny teased. At the end of the dock Johnny Robello and several of the other crew members were just finishing loading the technical equipment on the cabin cruiser that would motor them out to the small deserted island where the *Luscious* was moored.

"You guys all set?" Penny queried.

"Serge and Joe are already out there. Ross Herrington is letting us use his little outboard."

"Great!" Penny exclaimed. "Where's Max?"

"Should be here any minute." Johnny lugged the last heavy cable onto the cruiser. "You're early, Joel."

"I know." Joel scratched his dark head. "I wanted to . . . wanted to grab some extra rehearsal time with the sails, so I asked Penny if she'd mind if I hung around while you all set things up."

"No problem." Johnny accepted Joel's explanation with an easy smile.

Penny tugged at his arm, grateful that he had given Johnny a discreet reply. She didn't really mind if people found out about her and Joel, but it had been a considerate gesture on Joel's part and she appreciated it.

"Is Serge setting up on the *Luscious?*" Penny asked Johnny.

"Yep," said the older cameraman, nodding. "And Faye left a note for me at the desk saying that she was driving out with Tippy and Archie. The rest of the actors are being picked up right about now. But you know all that."

Penny ran down a checklist on her clipboard. "We sure have a great day to shoot."

"Sure do," Johnny yelled from the cruiser. "I'm going to head on out. Joel, you coming?"

In one smooth leap Joel was standing on the deck of the cruiser.

"I'm going to phone and make sure Max didn't oversleep," Penny called as Johnny revved up the motor. "Send the outboard back for me, okay?"

"Righto." Joel clicked his heels together and gave her a comical nautical salute.

Penny trotted back up the rickety dock and located a phone booth. It took forever for the New England Yacht Club to answer, and when they finally rang Max's room there was no one there.

"Great!" Penny mumbled. "He should be here any minute."

The smaller outboard was already waiting when she reached the end of the dock, so Penny, Irene, and several of the other actors who had arrived early piled into the boat and motored out to where the *Luscious* was moored. Once they began shooting they would use the cabin cruiser as a makeup and dressing room, and when it was necessary they would film some of the action taking place on board the sailing vessel from the cabin cruiser.

"It's so peaceful," Irene observed as the gleaming white prow of the *Luscious* came into view.

A perfect location, Penny thought, for the denouement of their current storyline. The *Luscious,* her sails still tied to her masts, was moored inside a gently curving cove. The water lapped against the rocky shore, and tall pines stood majestically in the distance.

"I'm glad I don't have much to do today," Irene confided as they piled out of the little outboard and walked toward the small tent that had been set up as a shelter from the scorching sun. "I'm going to just commune with nature."

"You have a pretty good scene to do with Joel." Penny's voice softened involuntarily as she spoke his name.

Irene gave Penny a knowing grin. "How's it going?"

"Okay," Penny replied, trying not to show her incredible excitement.

But Irene had not missed the glow of happiness that seemed to surround her tall, slender, sandy-haired friend. "I think it's fabulous that you and Joel have worked it out."

"We haven't . . . really," Penny protested, then, unable to contain her euphoria, her face broke into a smile. "Irene . . . I swear to you I never thought I'd feel this way!"

Irene hugged Penny impulsively. "As soon as we get back to New York I want to have you and Joel come to my apartment for dinner. And Pierre too, of course."

"Ah *oui*," teased Penny, "but of course!"

Serge and Johnny both called for her, and for the next forty-five minutes Penny was totally absorbed in figuring out the logistics of setting up. Periodically she glanced at her watch, then over her shoulder to see if the outboard was on its way back with Max. She solved the various problems the filming presented with an ease and clarity that she knew was impressing both Johnny and Serge. That made her feel even more terrific because both cameramen had been in the business for years and were respected professionals. She knew how quickly word spread, and she was certain that at least the technical work she had contributed to the remote would stand her in good stead in the future.

"Where is he?" Finally, at seven thirty when the rest of the actors, including Tippy, were ready and waiting to begin, Penny began to get really concerned about Max.

"He'll be here." Tippy looked anxiously off the starboard side of the *Luscious*.

"Coffee anyone?" Faye's outrageous bronze fluff emerged from the galley below.

"Maybe we should block the first scene." Penny's green eyes were troubled. Max had been so harassed and excitable lately. She was really concerned about him.

"Can you do a ship to shore?" She located the young man who

was representing Ross Herrington and acting as a lone crew member for the sailboat.

"Sure."

Penny sat next to him in front of the ship's radio, which was located down below next to the galley where Faye was brewing a pot of fresh coffee.

"Can't seem to get the right channel," Rick told Penny after several tries.

"Well, keep trying," Penny directed him, then went back up on deck to make sure Max had not come into view.

All of the actors and the fifteen additional extras who had been hired for the day were milling around in evening clothes. The first scene on the agenda was supposed to be after a raucous, drunken, all-night party. Penny stood alone, glancing nervously from her clipboard to the chattering actors to the stern of the ship where she hoped to spot the little outboard approaching.

"Coffee?" Joel, who was wearing a tuxedo with his tie askew, held out a plastic mug.

"Thanks." Penny took the cup absently and blew on the steamy liquid.

"He'll be here," Joel said reassuringly.

"We're losing time," Penny lamented. She looked up at the pristine blue sky. "And the light's going to change."

"Take it easy." Joel patted her shoulder, but she was not reassured.

Rick appeared from down below with news that he had contacted a boat that was heading for the New England Yacht Club and he had given them a message. Hopefully they would radio back within the next half hour.

"Too long!" Penny walked away from Joel and Rick. She paced for several minutes then made a decision. They would begin blocking the first setup. Max was sure to be here by the time they were ready to film it.

Using the small remote transistor radio that was fastened to her belt she radioed Johnny and Serge, who were waiting on the cabin cruiser just adjacent to the *Luscious.* Then after consulting with the stage manager, she called the cast together and told them she had decided to begin without Max. Immediately a vocal bedlam broke loose as everyone began expressing his or her personal opinion about Penny's decision.

"Hold it!" she called out authoritatively and was gratified by the immediate hush that fell over the crowd. "Max will be here. This is just a rehearsal . . . primarily for the cameras and to get sound levels."

Tippy intercepted her as she headed for the boat's stern to watch.

"You can't do this." Tippy put a restraining hand on Penny's arm.

"We have to begin." Penny's voice was sympathetic. "Anyway, like I said, I'm sure that Max will be here any minute."

Tippy's hand was trembling as she ran it through her hair, which was purposely disheveled for the first scene. "I know he planned on being here early," she confided to Penny. "That's why I decided to come with . . . Faye. I . . . you don't think he's had an accident?"

There was a note of hysteria in Tippy's voice, and Penny put her arm around the older woman to try to steady her. "He's fine. Believe me. Look, he'll be relieved to see that we've already blocked through this big crowd scene. It'll make things easier on him."

Tippy looked dubious. The last thing Penny needed was a dubious leading lady.

"You know how he worries about cost," Penny argued persuasively. "If we don't get this first scene down while the light is right, he's going to have to extend the remote and pay fifteen extras for an additional day's work. Not to mention the hassle of getting permission from the coast guard plus all the other red tape we went through."

Tippy gulped nervously and put her hand to her head.

"Are you all right?" Penny put both hands on Tippy's slender shoulders. Tippy nodded. "Please bear with me," Penny pleaded. "I think it's all for the best . . . for Max, if we go ahead."

Tippy walked away without a word, and Penny proceeded to block the entrances and exits of the fifteen formally attired extras. She had made no advance preparation so it was all improvisation. When they ran through the blocking for the first time, she was amazed at how smoothly she had managed to direct nearly twenty actors around the deck of the boat.

Although she was actually on board the *Luscious* directing the actors, it was necessary for her to project her imagination to the cabin cruiser where the cameras were located for this particular sequence. She was in constant touch with Serge and Johnny through the remote radio, and only twice did either of them suggest to her that she might consider a different camera angle.

"He's not in his room." Rick pulled her aside and whispered the bad news in her ear.

"What is it?" Tippy rushed over, sensing that something was wrong.

As Penny directed her attention to Tippy, Joel appeared, taking Tippy's hand in his in a supportive gesture. His eyes were full of concern for Tippy.

"It's nothing," Penny said. "Rick just got word that Max wasn't in his room. That's all."

"Let's do it." Irene joined the group. In her pink ruffled rumba dress she looked like a dimpled, sexy Kewpie doll. "We got the scene all blocked and we should just do it!"

"We're going to do it," Penny said firmly. She glanced briefly at Joel, but he remained silently noncommittal. She really could not tell what he was thinking.

But there was no time to dwell on Joel. Tippy was protesting, and there was the sense that she might balk at any minute. Archie's comments, while not in favor of going ahead with Penny at the helm, were circumspect. Of the principal actors only Irene was wholeheartedly and enthusiastically behind Penny.

But begin they did, and as the sun moved higher in the sky they proceeded to subsequent scenes, first blocking them and

166

then actually shooting the footage that would eventually be aired.

Penny's absorption was complete, and except for an occasional twinge of worry about Max she allowed only those details that concerned the script and its interpretation to enter her mind. Around ten thirty Rick emerged from the galley with another report received on the ship's radio. Max was suffering from acute stomach pains, but it was nothing serious. He had stopped at the doctor's en route to the location. He had been certain that the doctor could give him something to stop the severe abdominal cramping, but the doctor had put his foot down, fearing that the pains were symptoms of an imminent heart attack, and had insisted that Max go immediately to a hospital for tests.

"He's all right." Penny took Tippy aside, and without wondering why she had singled Tippy out to first hear the news, she explained the situation. Tippy went pale beneath her makeup, but she offered nothing in response other than a guarded thank you to Penny.

The news that Max Frost was in no serious trouble dissipated the tension, and Penny now felt totally free to enjoy her new role of director. Max would be proud—she knew he would. He had sent along words of encouragement. He did not feel obliged to work under duress because he believed that Penny could handle the scenes.

When they broke for lunch Penny had a conference with Serge and Johnny to see if they might have any tips, any criticism about the way she was calling shots. She listened attentively to their astute comments, and when they commenced shooting in the afternoon she was able to use their observations. She could feel herself growing, and that excited her. If she had any doubts at all about her desire or her aptitude for directing, by the end of the afternoon they were gone. She had been successful at communicating her wishes both to the crew and to the actors. She had never in her life spent such an exhilarating or satisfying day. As she rode back to shore in the cabin cruiser with Serge and Johnny, her mind was already leaping ahead to the next time. She had her film and she knew . . . she just knew it would be good. This was the break she had needed. Now it would be possible to get the sort of job she wanted, the job she really deserved!

"Congratulations!" Max was on the line when she ran into her room to answer the phone.

"I can't believe it," she gasped, still high from the experience. Her hair was a ratted mess, her face sunburned and salt-streaked from being out on the water nearly all day. Her white sweater had coffee dribbled down the front, and three of her fingernails were broken.

"I've had a couple of good reports—" Max began.

"How are you?" Penny burst in. "You don't know . . . you don't know how worried I was. How worried we all were."

"I'm better," Max said. "It seems I am the proud possessor of an ulcer."

"No!" Penny exclaimed.

"Better than a heart attack," Max countered.

"Yes," Penny agreed.

"Can you stop by my room before the party?" Max asked.

The party? My God, she had nearly forgotten the party. She had planned on going shopping for something special. She glanced at her watch as she finished talking to Max. If she hurried she would be able to fit everything in.

She flew back out of her room, her heart still thundering with a sense of accomplishment. For the last time she wound her way through the maze of narrow streets, and even though she was in a rush she could not help but pause to admire several of the eighteenth-century Georgian mansions. She and Joel would have to come back, she rhapsodized, perhaps over the Christmas holidays when the little village would be etched in frost.

First she returned to the cubbyhole of a bookstore where she purchased a beautifully engraved book on the art of scrimshaw for Joel. Several times he had mentioned his interest in the little articles which for centuries had been carved and engraved by whalemen out of either the tusks of walrus or whale ivory. What she would really love to give him was an actual scrimshaw piece, but her good sense prevailed over her economic optimism.

Still, she could not totally restrain herself from expressing her gratitude to the two cameramen, Irene, and of course Max. Having unearthed appropriate gift books for each of them, she left the bookstore loaded down. Actually, she felt so expansive that she would have liked to have bought gifts for everyone, for it seemed to her that the whole cast and crew including Tippy and, yes, even Archie had outdone themselves on her behalf.

Once again she passed the seductive little Victorian boutique, and once again she toyed with the idea of appearing as a vision in white. At length she grinned at her grimy, untidy appearance as it reflected back to her in the store window. Although she certainly didn't look that way at the moment, what she really felt like wearing was not some demure nineteenth-century frock but a slinky black silk dress she had purchased six months earlier but had never worn. She had been waiting for a special occasion, and what could be more special than tonight?

As she crossed the street a small shoe store caught her eye, and five minutes later she emerged having purchased a pair of strappy gold sandals with medium high heels. Next to the shoe store a beauty salon vied for her attention. The idea of letting someone else take care of her was enormously appealing after such a strenuous day, and for the next hour and a half Penny drifted somewhere between waking and sleeping while expert hands shampooed, trimmed, manicured, and pampered. When she finally roused herself to view the results she was pleasantly surprised. While the hairdresser had not altered her basically simple haircut, he had put in just enough hot rollers to give her sandy hair a bounce of curl then had pulled it gently back behind her ears, fastening it with a small barrette so that it fell softly against her slender neck.

An ideal style for her new black dress, she thought as she left the beauty salon on the run. Such an indulgence, but then she had saved time in the long run, for now she had only to soak in a hot tub and slip into her dress. It was still only seven o'clock, and the party didn't begin until nine. She would just drop her packages off at her room and then stop by to see Max as she had promised.

She was juggling her packages and fishing for the key to her room when Joel emerged from his room.

"Thanks . . ." Penny tucked her chin down to keep one of the packages from slipping out of her arms. It was not until Joel had thrown open her door and stood aside for her to enter that she noticed his grim expression.

"Something wrong . . . ?" She dropped her packages on the bed and looked anxiously into his face. When he did not reply, her eyes moved slowly back to the open door of her room. Just outside on the grass was a pile of luggage. Penny's face drew into a tight frown as she studied the rich chocolate-colored leather of the largest suitcase.

"Yours?" She looked back at Joel with dismayed eyes.

"I thought there'd be less traffic if I left tonight . . ." he stammered.

"You were leaving?" Without warning Penny's voice burst out of her in a loud, blatant inquiry. "You're really leaving?" she repeated in a shocked, quieter tone.

"I was going to phone you once you got back to the city," Joel offered rigidly as if that were all the explanation necessary.

"Why?" Penny shot him the question. "Are you sick? Is someone in your family sick? What's going on? I've been out celebrating. I . . ."

"Your hair looks nice," Joel offered awkwardly, and the incongruity of his response so infuriated Penny that she picked up one of her packages and threw it against the wall.

Penny looked around bewildered. She felt as if she had just been slugged in the stomach. "What do you mean my hair looks nice? You're getting ready to leave, and you have the audacity to stand there and calmly tell me my hair looks nice? Did you expect me to swoon at the compliment?"

170

Joel's dark eyes flashed and his mouth widened in a sardonic grin. *My God,* thought Penny, *he looks just like Buck.*

"I don't think this is the proper time to discuss it," he said coldly.

"You don't?" Penny eyed him with open hostility. What was this penchant he had for such abrupt changes?

"No, I think it would be better for us to talk once we're both back in the city . . . away from this place."

"I like this place." Penny felt her anger begin to waver. She jammed her hands into the pockets of her jeans and girded herself. She did not want to cry.

"What's going on?" Her voice was a hoarse whisper. "You were actually going to walk out after last night? I thought we were friends."

"You're upset," he remarked with a touch of agitation as if she had no right to be.

"Yes!" she cried. "Yes, I am upset. The other night you accused me of always being so calm . . . too calm. Well, here I am when I'm not calm. This . . . this has been the biggest, most incredible day of my life. I thought we'd be toasting my . . . my success and instead I find you sneaking out of my life."

"I think that's being a little overly dramatic," Joel said tightly, and it was the first time since she had really gotten to know him that Penny had detected such a patronizing tone to his voice. He wasn't himself. He was someone else. This was not the man she loved!

"Look, I wasn't sneaking out. I told you I was leaving you a note—"

"And did you really think"—Penny faced him squarely—"that I would simply read your little letter, toss it aside, and go out and have a wonderful time at the party? Did you really think—"

"Yes," Joel cut in, and he slammed the door shut with a ruthless motion. "Yes, that's what I thought. I saw you in action on board the *Luscious* today. After word came that Max was all right I'd never seen you more radiant."

171

A silence fell between them as Penny digested the full implication of his words. Her anger softened. She glanced at him, but he had moved to the French doors and was standing staring bleakly out at the shadowy ocean. It was simple then, wasn't it? He had been threatened by her involvement, by how happy and fulfilled she had been. Maybe he had been affected in much the same way as she had been affected having to watch his love scene with Tippy. It was true that she had ignored him all day. After she had assumed command, so to speak, she had spoken to him only in a professional capacity. Was he so vulnerable that his feelings had been hurt?

Penny stared hard at his massive shoulders. How would she have reacted if the situation had been reversed, if he had been called upon to perform some impromptu task and had simply ignored her? If she was honest she would have to admit that under the circumstances, because they were still uncertain of each other, still getting to know and understand each other's foibles, she too would have been wounded.

But she wouldn't have left! Her jaw tightened and the sympathy she had felt for him dried up. It had been her big day and he was ruining it.

He wheeled around on her suddenly. "It was very clear to me that your first love will always be directing."

"But I love you too," Penny cried in a frustrated voice.

"I don't want to be loved *too*!" Joel's tone was icy as he strode to the door.

"I didn't mean that!" Penny said, following him. "I didn't mean that the way it sounded. Why can't you understand?"

"I guess because at heart I am an ogre. Just like you thought I was. Selfish, rigid, incapable of loving . . . anyone."

"I would agree." Penny opened the door and held it for him. "I hope you have a pleasant drive back to New York."

Joel's magnetic eyes bored into her, but she did not flinch or waver from his gaze. "You'll probably just want to ignore the note. I left it at the desk for you."

"Yes, I probably will." She had jammed her hands back in the pockets of her jeans and was waiting for him to turn and leave so she could slam the door behind him. The depth of her fury almost frightened her. What was he waiting for? Why didn't he just turn around and leave?

"You're a pretty good judge of people, aren't you, Penny?" His tone was self-deprecating and bitter, but Penny had neither the heart nor the inclination to object.

She did not reply and finally she lowered her eyes. If he wanted her to contradict him he would have to wait a long time.

After a few moments she looked up. He was striding over the velvety lawn toward his car. A numbness came over her as she watched him put the luggage into the trunk and drive off. She turned to enter her room. She had forgotten to slam the door.

## CHAPTER THIRTEEN

Penny knocked lightly on Max's door. It was nearly dark, and the gas lamps dotting the lush grounds of the Yacht Club had just been turned on. Penny knocked again. Her face, still salt-streaked and unwashed, was melancholy. She shivered slightly then shook herself as she heard Max coming to the door.

"Hey . . . what's with you?" Max pulled her inside and studied her with a concerned expression.

"Nothing." Penny gave him a shaky smile.

"Don't tell me nothing." Max led her to a chair and poured her a glass of wine. "You should pardon the cliché, but you look like you just saw a ghost. You're not dressed. You're not going to the big doings?"

"Oh, I'm . . . going. You don't like my hair?" She waved her hand vaguely over her head.

"I've never seen you like this." Max crouched in front of her, and Penny noted that he was already dressed for the evening. Dimly she wondered what she had done for the past hour or so since Joel had left. Then she remembered that she had gone for a walk down on the beach. She had intended to get dressed before coming to see Max, but somehow that detail had slipped her mind.

"Honey . . . ?" Max peered at her.

"Thanks for trusting me today," she articulated after a moment. She sank back into the chair. Odd how meaningless that small triumph now seemed.

"Penny, you tell me what's bothering you, and that's an order." Max flushed and Penny felt a twinge of guilt for upsetting him. She started to shake her head, but one look at him told her he would not let up until she told him.

She opened her mouth to begin, but the words would not form. Then suddenly Max's arms were around her and she was sobbing.

"It's okay," he soothed. "Whatever it is, it's gonna be fine."

"I shouldn't be worrying you . . . with your ulcer and all." Penny buried her head in his bony shoulder.

"It's okay." Max patted her back. "It's not other people's troubles that get me down . . . it's my own. Now tell me what's going on. You were a terrific success today. What happened?"

"Joel." Penny wiped her eyes with Max's handkerchief.

"What the hell did he do?" Max sprang to his feet when a knock sounded at the door. "That'll be Tippy." He turned back to Penny. "I can ask her to come back later so we can talk."

Penny shook her head. "I don't care if she comes in."

"You sure?" Max inquired solicitously.

Tippy looked questioningly at Max as he opened the door for her. She was dressed for the evening in a chic white silk pants suit with a black strapless bodice.

"What's the matter, Pen?" Tippy knelt next to her and took one of her hands.

"It seems Mr. Sanborne is giving her a hard time," Max filled in, and Penny smiled wanly.

"He left." Penny looked from Tippy to Max.

"No!" Tippy exclaimed. "Why would he do that?"

"Something about the way I handled myself during the shoot today. Something," Penny continued tonelessly, "about not being able to . . . to share me with my work."

"That idiot!" Tippy jumped up and grabbed Max's arm emphatically. Max patted Tippy's hand but did not release it. Without thinking, he laced his fingers through hers and listened as she continued.

"I thought he was over that nonsense," Tippy addressed Penny. "He had a problem about competition when he was married to Monica. He had the same problem when he and I went together, but that was eons ago. Just the other night he told me he was determined not to let that get in his way where you were concerned."

"Well," Penny remarked drily, "he let it get in the way."

"Oh, that idiot," Tippy repeated with real concern. "I know him pretty well." The older woman viewed Penny sympathetically. "He's running scared."

"He's certainly running," Penny said bitterly.

Tippy gave her a sad smile of understanding. "He's afraid of his feelings . . . like many men." Tippy gave Max a brief smile, and it did not escape Penny's eye when he gave the tiny actress's hand a meaningful squeeze.

So it was Tippy and Max after all! Penny forced her attention back to what Tippy was saying.

"I know he probably behaved like a monster," said Tippy, "only he's not. You have a perfect right to be as upset and furious as you obviously are only . . . only I know how much he loves you. Joel and I are . . . well, he's my best friend." Tippy cast Max another warm smile. "I've never seen him so deeply in love as he is with you and for all the right reasons."

A rush of emotion brought new tears to Penny's eyes. The idea that Tippy Malone thought so highly of her was somehow deeply moving. And after all of those confusing, traumatic feelings she had had about Tippy. Someday, she thought, she would have to tell Tippy all about it.

"I know it's hard." Tippy handed Penny a fresh tissue. "You wanted to share this evening with him. By the way, you did a super job today. I'm sorry if I was a pill but. . . . Anyway, I know he'll come to his senses. I wouldn't be surprised if he hasn't already turned the car around and is heading back to Marble-head."

"You gotta come to the party." Max let go of Tippy's dainty hand with a final squeeze. "Tippy and I will wait for you while you get dressed."

"Okay." Penny dragged herself to her feet.

"Don't write Joel off," urged Tippy as she followed Penny to the door. "Even if he is bullheaded enough to drive back to New York, I know he'll come around."

"I feel better." Penny leaned down and kissed the tiny woman on the cheek. "Thanks, Tippy."

"I'm rooting for you both," Tippy said and smiled. As Penny walked off toward her own room, she suddenly ran after her.

"Would you like to use my car to drive back to New York tonight?" Tippy offered.

"That's generous," Penny responded, and before she could decline, Tippy had opened her evening purse and was pressing keys in her hand.

"Max and I are going to take a few days together." She looked evenly at Penny.

"I hope it works out." Penny nodded meaningfully.

"We fought it for as long as we could," Tippy whispered.

"You don't have to explain," Penny replied softly, and Tippy gave her a grateful nod. "I probably won't use your car . . ."

". . . but if you do just leave it at the garage across from the studio. Max and I will be back by Wednesday." Tippy threw Penny a kiss as she turned back toward Max's room.

How incongruous, thought Penny, that the woman who had been the source (or so she had thought) of so much uncertainty and, yes, jealousy, had in the end given her so much comfort and encouragement. Back in her room Penny tossed Tippy's car keys on her bed and stared at them. What a generous gesture that had been!

She had always liked Tippy, always respected the way she

conducted herself at the studio, but now her esteem for the older actress had deepened. No doubt she and Max had gone through a lot of anguish over their love affair. Well, she hoped it worked out for Tippy and Max. Now that she thought of it she must have been blind not to have understood the deep bond between them.

She stripped off her salty work clothes, rolled them into a ball, and jammed them in the dirty clothes corner of her suitcase. Tippy and Joel. They really were good friends. Suddenly Joel's loyalty to Tippy struck her in a new light. He had not deserted the friendship even at two thirty in the morning. Knowing Tippy as she now felt she did, Penny realized that something pretty upsetting must have been going on. Nausea, fainting . . . was it possible that Tippy was pregnant?

Penny stepped gingerly into the hot tub and slid down into the fragrant bubbly water. Of course, it made absolute sense! Tippy had all the symptoms and Max . . . Max had said his life was a mess and. . . . No wonder they were all so upset—no wonder Tippy needed to talk to someone in the middle of the night.

Penny dabbed at her face with the washcloth, being very careful not to completely undo her new hairstyle. Not that it mattered. She felt a twinge of regret at the prospect of spending the evening without Joel. She closed her eyes and tried to remember Tippy's encouraging words. Talking with Max and Tippy had helped enormously. At least she was breathing now and not in a stupor of depression. Now that the shock of Joel's negative reaction to her success was wearing off she was able to think more clearly. Of course she would not be able to tolerate his erratic behavior indefinitely, but Tippy had seemed to understand that. If Tippy was right, and somehow Penny trusted the other woman's opinion of Joel, he would find a way of dealing with his jealousy in a positive manner.

Jealousy? Penny soaped one long tanned leg with a curious expression. In a way Joel's reaction was precisely that—jealousy. He had become apprehensive and fearful because he had witnessed how compelling and enthralling she had found her work.

He couldn't have had a more possessive reaction if Penny's attentions had been directed toward another man.

The fact that Joel was considering giving up acting himself had probably complicated his reactions, too. Penny's stomach constricted into a knot as she thought of the hopelessness she had read in his dark eyes. There was no doubt in her mind how miserable he had been. Sorting things out now she saw that his anger had never been really directed at her but only at himself.

"Dear God, let him be careful!" Penny's face was twisted with concern as she climbed out of the tub and began to towel off. Any resentment or anger she had felt toward him melted away in the face of her distress over his well-being. The Friday night traffic would be heavy, they had had little sleep, and he was probably exhausted from working in the sun all day.

Why hadn't she stopped him? Tears sprang to her eyes as she sprinkled a jasmine-scented talcum powder on her body. She was in a new panic now as she ran to the phone and called Max.

"Max Frost's room," Tippy answered after several rings.

"Sorry," Penny apologized straight away without identifying herself. "He'll drive safely, won't he, Tippy? I'm kicking myself now for not being more understanding."

"Don't you dare kick yourself," was Tippy's sharp reply. "You didn't behave badly . . . *he* did."

"I know." Penny fought back tears. Knowing that it had been his fault and not hers did not make things better. Nothing would make things better except to be in his arms and know that he was safe.

"Don't let your imagination run away with you," cautioned Tippy. "Believe me, Joel is the best driver I know. He used to drive in races. Also . . . even though he's upset, he's not crazy. He won't take any chances on the road."

Penny sighed audibly.

"Hang in there," Tippy advised. "Max is resting. Shall I come by for you or do you want to meet me at the party?"

"I'll meet you . . ." Penny felt the emptiness closing in. "Max . . . is all right?"

"He'll be over later. He needs rest. Now, don't worry!" Tippy gave one last caveat before hanging up.

Lethargically Penny slipped into black lace panties and a matching bra. She sat on the edge of the bed fastening the straps of her new gold sandals.

She switched on the radio and the sound of a muted clarinet moaned out a blues tune. The melancholy music only intensified her yearning for him, but she did not turn it off. What could she do? It was the helplessness that was killing her because she could not reach him. He was incommunicado on the road. It would be another six hours before he would be in his New York apartment. The idea of waiting six hours to hear the sound of his voice was intolerable.

Tippy was right, of course. She shouldn't blame herself. Only what was she going to do in the meantime? On impulse she rummaged in her bag until she found the list of phone numbers for the cast, then she picked up the phone and dialed his number in New York.

Her heart was pounding and nervous dots of perspiration formed on her upper lip. Her eyes grew bright as she heard a click on the other end of the line.

"This is Joel," came the familiar smooth baritone. "I'm not able to come to the phone at the moment. In a few seconds there will be a beep. If you'd like you can leave a message."

Penny clutched the receiver with both hands. Under the best of circumstances she hated those obnoxious answering machines. Always she suffered an attack of nerves before leaving her message, and tonight she felt as though she were sitting on a lighted keg of dynamite as she waited for the aforementioned beep.

"This is Penny." She threw one leg over the other and hunched her body into the receiver as she spoke. "It's uh . . . nine thirty Friday. I . . . I feel wretched . . . I . . . I miss you."

She paused and looked wildly around the room. The seconds were ticking away. In a moment the little beep would sound again and cut her off.

"I want to know you're safe. If you get in tonight would you please phone me here at the Yacht Club? I . . . I'll be back in New York by three tomorrow afternoon. You have my number. It feels strange not having you next door."

She replaced the receiver slowly before the beep sounded. Now what?

She stretched her long bare legs out in front of her, then finally stood up and walked over to the armoire to locate the black silk dress. It seemed almost that she could feel his presence in the room.

She removed the dress from the hanger and slipped the fine, sensuous fabric over her head. Of all the moments they had shared, the one that kept creeping up on her to infuse her body with an almost excruciating longing was the night they had moved silently in this very room, undressing and preparing for bed.

Penny looked at herself in the full-length mirror. The black silk dress clung to her gentle curves. The effect was both sophisticated and sexy. She studied herself thoughtfully, and it occurred to her that it was odd that she didn't look particularly miserable. She cocked her head to one side as if to make sure she was seeing herself correctly.

"Let's get on with it." She turned away from the mirror and went into the bathroom to put on a skin moisturizer and some lip gloss. She dabbed some of the jasmine-scented perfume behind her ears and fastened gold drop earrings on her lobes. Actually she was starving. And with good reason; she had existed for an entire day on coffee and one small raspberry yogurt.

She started for the door, stopped, and returned to locate the key to her room. Why was she procrastinating when she was practically weak with hunger? She looked nostalgically around the room then found herself outside on the terrace.

The hunger she felt twirling in the pit of her stomach had more to do with Joel Sanborne than lack of food. She sighed against the night, heard the tide lapping at the shore below. *You're there?*

Was that what he had said that first night. *You're there, aren't you?*

Penny smiled softly as she tried the words out, measuring their timbre against the silence of the night. "You're there, aren't you?"

"I am," came a voice from the other side of the trellis.

"Joel . . . ?" Penny started.

"I'm a fool," said his lonely voice.

"You're here?" she questioned, scarcely believing it could be possible.

"Do you think you can ever forgive me?" came his hoarse reply.

"Oh, Joel!" She was near tears. She felt like tearing down the damned trellis with her bare hands. "Didn't you leave? Didn't you . . . I saw you get in your car and drive off."

There was a long silence. "I know," he said faintly.

"What happened?" Penny pressed against the vines.

"You won't believe it," he said glumly, and she could picture the woebegone look on his face.

"Try me." She could almost taste the bitter green leaves that ran up the trellis.

"I got lost."

"What?" Penny exclaimed.

"I couldn't find my way out of Marblehead."

"No!" Penny burst out laughing. Her legs were trembling, and she pulled a chair over and sat down. "Sorry . . . I . . . I didn't mean to laugh."

There was another long silence, then she heard a low chuckle. "I got lost. I knew I was upset but . . . ."

"This is crazy." Penny wasn't sure if it was hysteria, but whatever it was, she could not stop laughing. "I'll meet you halfway."

But by the time she opened her door Joel was standing there with a roguish grin on his handsome face and a bouquet of gardenias in his hands.

A rush of timidity swept over Penny as she detected a flicker of embarrassment in his dark eyes. She had never seen him so startlingly handsome as he was at that moment. He was dressed to perfection in a dark suit, the crisp white collar of his shirt almost glowing in contrast to his dark skin. He thrust the bouquet of gardenias into her hand and walked to the center of her room, still smiling roguishly to cover his discomfort.

Penny's mouth was parched as she closed the door and turned back to him. For a moment they stood staring at each other.

"I'd better put these in water." Penny flushed as she scurried toward the bathroom to perform the task. The sound of the water gushing from the sink faucet was a relief from the awkward silence that had fallen between them once they were face to face. Penny stuffed the lovely bouquet into her one and only glass, then returned to find Joel rooted to the same spot.

"They look all right here?" She placed the flowers next to her bed and turned to him. He nodded sheepishly, and Penny directed her full attention to situating the glass . . . as if that were the most important thing on her mind.

"You really got lost?" She made a nervous stab at conversation.

"First time in my life," Joel admitted with a glimmer of humor. "I always prided myself on my flawless sense of direction. I'm the kind of person who knows where he is *all* the time. I scoffed at those jokes about how difficult it was to find your way out of Marblehead, and I think I'm the only one here who never got lost . . . until tonight."

His dark eyes moved relentlessly over her face as he spoke. She had never seen him so serious.

"All of those one-way streets . . ." He took a step toward her, and Penny felt a pause in her breathing before it resumed again at an accelerated rate.

"I've never seen so many one-way streets." He reached for her hand and held it warmly as his brow wrinkled in a moment of consternation. "I must not have wanted to leave Marblehead. After several ill-fated attempts to locate a one-way street which

183

was going the way I wanted it to go I began to see things more clearly. I was leaving town . . . because I was afraid of . . ."

He paused and stared at her hand. She wanted to help him out of the awkward moment but there was nothing she could do. If she reached out to him now and drew his face toward hers, if they kissed and touched and lost themselves in the joy of their mutual passion, he might never find those words that were so difficult for him to speak.

"It was easier for me to talk when we were separated by that damned trellis," he confessed with a wry smile.

"Maybe you want to go back to your side . . . I'll go outside on my terrace and . . ." Penny was not altogether kidding and he knew it.

"Why are words sometimes so difficult?" he asked.

Penny shrugged. "They are. I know they are."

"You know I love you," Joel drew her closer, and she rested the palms of her hands against his chest. Beneath the jacket, the shirt, she felt his heart pounding as urgently as hers.

"I know." She rested her cheek against the thudding sound and put her arms around him gently, soothing him.

"Sometimes love is not enough," he said thickly.

Penny felt a new iciness clutching at her heart, but she continued moving her hand up and down his back in the same soothing pattern. How she wanted his hands to glide over her body, to feed the fires she was struggling to hold in abeyance.

"I mean . . ." he continued in a hesitant voice, "I mean to say I love you isn't enough. Even to mean it . . . isn't always enough. A person has to be able to act with love and constancy. I know I failed you today. I should have been able to be happy seeing you so excited, so . . . so brilliant. Yes, you were brilliant and . . . and not only because of the choices you made for shots and angles but because of the tact and respect with which you treated everyone."

Penny tried to pull away, to object that he did not need to compliment her. He pushed her head gently back against his chest and continued. He seemed to find it easier speaking to her when they were touching only. Penny closed her eyes as she listened to his deep voice. She knew the expression on his face, knew his dark eyes were cloudy with a trace of sadness.

"I guess I couldn't handle it because you were treating me like everyone else. That hurt."

"I didn't mean . . ." Penny started to protest, but he silenced her with a gentle squeeze.

"It scared me when I realized that I was going to have to share you with your talent. And you are talented. I saw that today along with everyone else. It was a piggish response, I know—"

"Joel," Penny interrupted finally, "I could have made things easier."

"Of course," he nodded. "You mean by pampering me. By running over and holding my hand every few minutes to make sure my feelings weren't getting hurt. I don't think either one of us wants that."

Penny nodded. "I see your point."

"What I discovered," said Joel, "as I was making all those wrong turns trying to get out of Marblehead, was that one of the reasons I love you so much is because of this fierce dedication you have to your work. The very thing that threatened me was one of the things I most admire about you."

"I love you." Penny pulled away from him and gazed into his thoughtful face.

"And . . . you forgive me?" Joel's lean face was still earnest.

"I forgave you"—Penny glanced at her watch—"about an hour ago."

Joel smiled. "That's about when I decided there was no getting out of Marblehead . . . at least not without you."

Now for the first time he relaxed, and the familiar hungry look came into his eyes as they traveled down her black clad body.

"We have a party to go to." He gave her an insinuating smile.

"I know." Penny reached out for him, and as she felt the length of his lean, muscular body pressing into her she sighed.

"I missed you," he murmured as his fingertips gently traced her silky curves.

185

Penny's lips parted as she raised her mouth to his. He smiled at her eagerness and ran his forefinger around her lips, teasing her.

"Some dress," he breathed as she nipped hungrily at his finger. "I never figured you for a slinky black dress."

"I have other surprises." Penny felt the intoxication of his presence. Her legs felt rubbery, her entire body longed for him.

"I'm sure you have many surprises." Joel lowered his mouth to hers and covered her parted lips with his warm, moist mouth. His breath tasted vaguely of wine, but it was a delicate fruity taste that only heightened her desire. She widened her mouth wanting to drink in every taste, every drop of him. His lips felt soft as they encased her mouth. She moved her hand to his face and felt his smooth, clean-shaven cheek, then unable to control the flaming need he had set off in her, she moved her body against his until his tongue shot inside her mouth and delved into her.

He had come back and that was all that mattered. Tomorrow they would return to New York City and somehow they would learn to deal with their problems. She knew they would.

Her body seemed to ooze into his as his kisses grew more demanding and his hands guided her hips in a slow rocking motion.

"Such a nice dress"—he drew away from her, bleary-eyed—"I hate to see it go."

Penny smiled languidly as he ran his hands over her breasts. He was breathing heavily. One hand lingered lovingly over her left breast, but his eyes never left her face.

"You really do forgive me?" His voice was choked with desire.

"Doesn't it seem that way?" Penny felt a shiver of ecstasy as his hand slipped beneath the thin silk and fondled her breast.

"I want to make love to you . . ." Joel's words were like a plea, and they set off a spasm of erotic anticipation that seemed to shake her whole body. "I want to feel your breasts against me, want to touch you . . . make you laugh . . . I don't ever want to behave as foolishly as I did tonight."

Joel let out a muffled groan as his hand continued to caress her creamy breast. "Do you believe me?"

The desire raging through her was making it difficult to breathe, let alone to talk. Penny nodded.

Joel molded her breast into his large palm until Penny yearned for his hands to sweep the length of her body, creating those delicious sensations that only he seemed capable of arousing in her. Her staunch nipple swelled beneath his touch. He placed the other hand in the small of her back and brought her up against him. Slowly he lowered his face toward hers to catch her parted lips in light teasing kisses. He manipulated her breast as his tongue flicked like a serpent in and out of her mouth. Half laughing she tried to catch it.

"Tease . . . !" Joel withdrew his hand from beneath the flimsy silk dress.

"Look who's talking?" Penny taunted him slyly.

He leered at her hungrily, then reached in his pocket. "I bought you something." He handed her the small box he had removed from his jacket.

"What . . . ?" Penny tried to shake off the dazed, intoxicated feeling his inquisitive fingers had set off. Although he had removed his hand from her breast she continued to feel its warmth. He guided her to the bed and made her sit on the edge. Her body felt like a river; she was a flowing ribbon of desire, yearning for him. He placed the box in her outstretched hand, and she stared at it as if something so solid as a box had no meaning for her.

Joel smiled softly. "Open it."

"You've taken away my . . . my . . ." Penny stammered as she fumbled with the narrow white ribbon.

"Open it," Joel repeated, and as she untied the bow he bent down to unfasten her gold sandals.

"I can't concentrate," Penny cried half laughing.

"You don't have to concentrate." Joel grinned up at her.

"You're taking off my sandals," Penny cried in mock alarm. "We have a party to go to."

She felt his cheek rub against the smooth calf of her leg. Then as his hand traveled up onto the inside of her thigh, she let out a little squeal.

"Joel, it's . . ." Penny gasped as she removed the delicately carved piece of ivory from the box. Joel stood up and bent over her, smiling proudly at the meticulously executed design that was carved into the ivory scrimshaw.

"It looks almost like the *Luscious.*" Penny squinted at the detailed miniature of the old sailing vessel. The scrimshaw piece was very old; she knew it was incredibly valuable. She turned it over in her hand and saw that a dainty gold loop had been secured to the back so that it could be worn as a necklace. She looked up at him with tears in her eyes.

"I don't believe in engagement rings," Joel said softly. "I thought this was so much more appropriate."

Penny blinked unbelievingly. "What are you saying?"

Joel chuckled at her bluntness. "That's what I like about you, kiddo, right to the point."

He sat down on the bed next to her and took her hand. "I'm saying that I want this to work. I think you and I have a shot here at something pretty special and I don't want to lose it. I don't want to lose you. Ever."

"You mean"—Penny's eyes were sparkling with laughter and with tears—"you mean . . . this is not just another remote."

"I mean"—Joel nuzzled her ear—"that there is nothing at all remote about the way I feel about you."

Penny turned to him with a tremulous smile. "I love you so much and . . . this . . ." She glanced back at the piece of engraved ivory. "Funny, I did a bit of shopping for you. Nothing so extravagant but . . ."

Joel's eyes followed her as she padded across the room and returned with a large rectangular package tied in a big red bow. He opened it carefully, and his face lit up when he saw the book that detailed the history of the art of scrimshaw.

"I guess we're mostly of one mind." Joel smiled approvingly. "There's something else."

"I don't know if I can stand anything else." Penny stood in front of him with her hands on his shoulders.

"You were right," he said, "when you said it didn't matter if I decided to quit the business. I mean, as far as *we* were concerned. You were also right when you suggested that it might just be time for me to abandon dear old Buck Handlin and go on to other things."

"You've decided to quit the show?" Penny questioned.

"I've decided to take a leave of absence," he said with a satisfied smile.

"That's a great idea!" Penny sat on his lap and gave him a hug. "Maybe you'll get a job playing a decent sort for a change."

"Would you like that?" Joel rubbed his hand against her softly rounded stomach.

"I would recommend you." Penny did not hide the pleasure his touch gave her.

"As a lover?" Joel reached around to the zipper at the back of the black silk dress.

"As a lover, yes." Penny shivered as the back of her dress opened. "And as a friend."

"Ummm." Joel smacked his lips as he gently pulled down the top of the dress and took in the fullness of her breasts as they spilled out of the lacy black bra.

"We're going to be late for dinner." Penny smiled dreamily as his dark eyes devoured the pink nipples that peeked through the delicate lace. He rubbed his mouth across the lacy fabric, and her already firm nipples tingled with pleasure.

"As long as we get to the party in time to squelch all of those horrible rumors." Joel gave her a devilish grin as he reached around her slender torso to unhook the flimsy fabric. "Yes, we'll arrive just in time for the last dance." As the bra fell to the floor he placed his warm mouth over one hard, rosy nipple. He sucked deeply and Penny felt a response quicken in her stomach. He rolled his tongue around the rosy bud then moved to the other breast.

"If that's all right with you?" He looked up at her after a moment and she nodded breathlessly.

"Suddenly the lady is very agreeable," Joel teased, and he held out his hand to help her keep her balance as she stepped out of the black dress. She stooped to pick it up, but he stopped her. She watched as he hung the dress on a hanger, and when he turned back to her she flushed slightly. She looked down at her black lace panties then back at him with a questioning smile.

Joel returned her smile and began to loosen his tie. "I like black lace."

Penny did a little wiggle and Joel clasped her around the waist and rubbed against her. He slipped both hands beneath the brief panties and cupped her behind firmly. Penny felt a boiling sensation surge through her, and her mouth sought his in a demanding kiss. As he molded her into him she infused him with her own fire.

"My God," he groaned, "what have I gotten myself into?"

Penny's fingers moved expertly to unbutton his shirt, and with her mouth still moving on his she helped him out of his shirt and proceeded to unfasten his belt. His hands on her hips were more insistent now, for he was gripped by a sense of urgency she had created in him. He broke away from her and swiftly completed removing his trousers.

Penny moved to him and wrapped her arms around his neck. She placed her hands on his hips and threw her head back as he nuzzled into her breasts. Then there were no more barriers that could hold them back. Joel whisked her off her feet, and after he had removed the scant black panties he inched slowly toward his goal. Penny cried out several times as he led her on a search for new erotic pleasures. He seemed bent on leaving nothing untouched. He was everywhere at once, she thought, feeling his hands rummaging through her once perfectly coiffed hair. She luxuriated in the liberties he took and endeavored to keep pace with his vitality which seemed to know no bounds.

At length they matched each other perfectly, arriving at an achingly beautiful conclusion that brought tears to her eyes.

Penny's face was flushed and rosy with the healthy glow of love. She nestled her head in his damp chest and listened to the thud of his heart, smiling as it gradually grew slower and more sedate, she thought.

After a while Joel turned to her with an amused smile. "Absence makes the heart grow fonder, is that it?"

"Something like that." Penny nipped impishly at his hardened nipple.

He rolled over and hugged her impulsively. "It's just incredible how much I love you, Penny Phillips. I know it's an odd thing to say but . . . I want everyone to know."

"You do?" Penny thrilled to his confession as he cradled her in his arms.

"Especially Tippy . . . you don't mind my saying that?" He looked at her tentatively.

Penny shook her head firmly. "I talked to Tippy while you were driving around Marblehead."

"You did?" Joel was surprised.

Penny nodded. "She calmed me down. I like her."

"You were mad." Joel chuckled, remembering. "You threw a package."

"I know." Penny felt all bubbly as she recalled. "I never did that before."

"We're even," Joel whispered. "I never got lost and you never threw things. It's an auspicious beginning."

"Yes, it is." Penny rolled over on her back and drew him down toward her. For several moments they lay in silence, their glistening eyes drinking in the wonder each read in the other's face. There was the rustle of the soft sea breeze outside the window and the measured unison of their breathing which seemed to fill the silence in Penny's little room with the rarest of music.

This, thought Penny, was the deepest bond of all . . . deeper than the words, deeper than the laughter, and deeper even than the promises they had given to each other. The silent wonder she read in Joel Sanborne's eyes would be with her forever.

191

*LOOK FOR NEXT MONTH'S*
*CANDLELIGHT ECSTASY ROMANCES* ®